1

DANGEREUSE:

Grandmother of Eleanor of Aquitaine

BY J.P. REEDMAN

3

CHAPTER ONE

"Amauberge!"

My nursemaid's peevish cry rang out across the bailey, and I dashed to hide behind the spiny bushes growing up the castle wall. I was glad it was spring and the greenery thick and lush and concealing, otherwise my bright red hair, falling free to my waist, would flame like a beacon and I would be caught.

"Amauberge!" Sour old Betrana stalked by, near enough I could smell her aroma of lavender and sweat. Her face was the colour of a thunderhead beneath her starched white cap. "I know you are here. You had best show yourself, you minx or they will be Hell to pay! You are far too old to play these childish games! Your Lady Mother wishes to see you and she will be most displeased by this delay."

In my hiding spot against the lichen-splotched wall, I rolled my eyes. My mother, Lady Gerberga, was nearly as bad as Betrana—always chiding me for scraped knees and dirty gowns. "You have a dirty mouth too, girl!" she had even cried once, when I had sworn a particular florid oath after enduring a good hour of chastisement about a torn and muddied hem. She had sent me to bed without bread that evening, but I had amused myself by dropping some bright coloured pebbles I had collected for just such an occasion on the heads of anyone who passed below my tower room.

"AMAUBERGE!" Betrana roared again. Her mouth had grown cavernous, like a dragon's, and her cheeks were mottled puce. A thread of spittle clung to the corner of her lips. Despite myself, I began to feel a little uneasy. What if she should collapse and die of an apoplectic fit from so much yelling? It happened; I had seen an old market trader die in such a manner. I would be responsible for her demise, should she succumb, and hence I would surely go to Hell to be pronged by demon's burning tridents for eternity.

I sighed. I had better give myself up and take my punishment…

"*Yaahh*, Betrana, you silly goose! I was here all along!" I sprang from the bushes, showering greenery, my hair snarled with twigs and leaves, a bleeding scratch on my forearm where the thorns had gouged my flesh.

Betrana jumped in alarm, hand pressed theatrically to her enormous bosom. "Oh, you wicked girl, Amauberge! You frightened me. It is hot; you've made my heart race…Jesu have mercy, and look at you, leaves stuck all over you as if you were some evil pagan forest imp. Whatever gets into you? I swear it must be the Devil himself! Oh, my giddy head, I must sit down…"

I was now genuinely concerned that I had done her a mischief, and I was sorry for it, for although she irritated me when she dogged my steps like a hound, underneath I liked her truly. She would sneak sweetmeats from my parents' table and give them to me to devour under the cover of my bed. Sometimes she even helped fix the gowns I ruined on an almost daily basis.

"Here…let me help you. I am sorry, Betrana," I said, leading her to an old, lichenous stone seat that stood against the firm base of one of the towers, an arch of flowering brambles making a natural canopy. It was shaded there, too, the shadow of the squat tower casting a long black streak over the summer-parched grass.

Betrana slumped down, wheezing breathily and rubbing her arm across her sweat-dimpled brow. After a few moments, she recovered, her breath slowing and her cheeks losing that ominous purple hue. I was glad she was fine again...but now I must find out why she was so determined to find me, and if I would get punished for hiding...

"Why did you come looking for me, Betrana?" I asked, toying with the end of a strand of hair. It burned brightly in the sunlight.

"Why were *you* hiding in a bush?" she asked, sternly. "Do not question *me*, young mistress."

I had no real answer to give. None that she had not heard a thousand times. I merely enjoyed an hour's freedom from learning stitchery and dancing and all that other nonsense. I understood I had to learn it, as did all good ladies of quality, but not this moment, in the height of summer, with the sun shining like a coin and the flowers blooming...

I rubbed a little at my nose. It was peeling. I had caught the sun and it was sore. Betrana saw too and glowered. "For Jesu's sake, Amauberge! You should not be out in the heat of the day. You do not want to be brown like some field labourer, do you? Even worse, with your red hair, you might get a crop of ugly freckles. Then men will think you have had the pox and you won't have any suitors!"

"Maybe I am fine with that!" I tossed my unruly locks back over my shoulders and wrinkled my red nose. "Maybe I won't ever marry, as my choice."

"Perish the thought the poor nuns would ever have to deal with a hoyden like you," huffed Betrana, shaking her head.

"Nuns! I would never join the old crows in a convent," I said defiantly. "I would become a...a lady knight who would ride about on a fine white horse slaying dragons and paynims. Or if a knight is impossible, a lady such as Matilda of Tuscany, who was known as 'the Great Countess' and ruled in her own right! No one told her what to do!"

A corner of Betrana's mouth quirked up. "Even Countess Matilda married, though…and not to a husband of her own choice. Neither of her marriages was a success. The first was to a man called Godfrey the Hunchback."

"Yes, I know all about the Hunchback," I said imperiously, "but Matilda got rid of him, did she not? As for her second husband, Welf…" I smirked. "Well, *that* was scandalous, wasn't it? He was so scared of her using witchcraft on him that he refused to share her bed. Matilda was furious and laid herself on a table, naked as the day she was born, and had Welf brought to her chamber. She told him that all the delights revealed to him were his and his alone, and he need fear no sorcery. Well, he stood with his mouth agape like a loon, and in frustration she slapped him and called him a monster and a worm…and even rotted seaweed!"

Betrana fanned her big, round face, looking a little flushed again. "Amauberge, wherever did you hear that dreadful story?"

"From some noblewomen visiting mother a few months back," I said, smug. "The ladies were all abuzz with it. They'd imbibed too much wine and could talk of little else."

Betrana poked a fleshy finger at me. "Your mother would never have let such crudities be spoken in front of her child. You were eavesdropping, weren't you, Amauberge?"

Her accusation was true. The ladies had gathered in the garden and I had hidden behind the grape vines, plucking the odd ripe grape to wet my dry mouth as they gossiped about things I only half-understood. A glorious, lazy afternoon with no tutors.

It seemed Betrana had already made up her mind about my guilt anyway, for she did not wait for me to answer her question. She pulled her bulky form up, brushing down her bleached linen apron. "Enough of this foolishness. Her ladyship will be wondering what has become of us. It was she who sent me to find you. A special visitor is coming to the castle."

I shrugged, bored. "Visitors frequently do. It's a castle, a landmark clear to see for miles around."

"Well, for whatever reason, your mother has asked that you be dressed in suitable attire and made…ladylike. So, come, no more dallying. Time is pressing."

She began to waddle toward the steps leading up into the keep and I followed, curious and a little alarmed. Who could this guest be, for whom I must look especially presentable?

I was dressed in my very best gown, the one mother said she would beat me over if I stained or tore it. The dress was loose and flowing, wrought of sky-blue silk from the Moorish lands in Andalusia. It was worth a fortune, mother liked to remind me, and not only was I supposed to not ruin it, I was also not supposed to grow too stout to wear it either. Tallness could be fixed with extra panels inserted of lesser material, but any fatness would distort the dress and pop the seams. I wondered how this would work soon, as my chest had swelled considerably in the past few years, but a skilled seamstress had managed to loosen the bodice adequately without ruining the gown's lines, after Betrana had first wrapped me in a tight linen chemise that made me looked disappointingly shapeless.

"We don't want your wares on display like some harlot in the marketplace," Betrana said ominously when I complained I could not breathe from the tight fit. "Now stand still and hold in your belly for the belt." She grabbed a silvered ceinture from a chest, looping it around my middle and knotting it tightly; sparkling tassels jiggled as I moved.

She stepped back, looking me up and down and admiring her handiwork. "There, now you look like a girl and not some imp. Pity about your burnt red nose, but there is no helping that. The only thing now is to fix your hair."

She lunged at me with a brush and I moaned and grizzled as she attacked my hair as a stableboy might go at a horse's tail. Despite her puffing and huffing, soon it was bound in a great thick braid mixed with gaudy ribbons.

"Just one more thing, for a nice finishing touch," Betrana said, and she took up a small silver circlet my father had gifted me at Christmastide and placed it carefully on my brow. "There...a proper lady. Now go. I believe your parents are already giving greetings to their guest in the Hall."

I entered the Great Hall of our little castle—it was smoky, as ever, the firepit in the centre burning brightly. The haze was a bit worse than usual; some fool must have brought in logs that were too green. Smoke coiled up to exit from the small vent in the roof, amongst the ashy carved angels that stared down from above, looking more demonic than heavenly with their smudged faces.

Upon the dais sat my father, Bartelmy de l'Isle Bouchard, and my mother Gerberga de Blaison. Both wore exquisite clothing, even as I. Cabochons gleamed on belts and headbands; silks rustled and sleeves drifted like wings. They were chatting animatedly with a man I had never met before. All three held goblets and looked very merry and congenial.

The stranger was tall and dressed even finer than my parents, his long, scarlet tunic trimmed with gold threads that made curlicue patterns. He was perhaps five years older than me—he was beardless and had sleek near-black hair to the shoulder. His skin was sun-bronzed and I caught a glimpse of bright blue eyes as he laughed and jested with my parents. I guessed he was someone of higher rank for them to be so cordial to one so young.

"Ah, here you are, Amauberge." Father turned in my direction, his fur-lined cloak swinging, making him appear like a great bear. "Come and meet, Lord Aimery, Viscount of Châtellerault."

I approached the dais, giving a deep and, I hoped, graceful curtsey. I had thought I would be bored stiff in the presence of my father's guest…but to my surprise, Aimery intrigued me. I did not know any young men, having had but one younger baby brother who died in infancy, and certainly none I was allowed to speak to. Most of those I saw daily were either stableboys with straw-matted hair and horse muck beneath their nails or else they were castle guards or soldiers, rough-hewn and tousled, their teeth often broken from fights, their eyes hard and restless. Aimery was…refined. And a Viscount. And, dare I say it, rather handsome.

"So, this is the famed Amauberge," said Aimery. "She is as beautiful as the rumours say."

"There are rumours about me?" I blurted, eyes wide. Mother cast me a terrible look.

Aimery laughed. "Only good things, I sure you, Lady Amauberge. That you are fair of face and full of grace and wit."

I dimpled and flushed, pleased but trying not to show it. It would not do to appear vain.

"Although I have also heard..." Aimery pretended to frown, but I could tell it was a pretended frown, for his lips were upturned even though his brow lowered, "that the entrancing Amauberge is also wild as an Amazon and loves hawks, hounds and horses as much as any lad. Better than the gentle arts more appropriate for maidens."

Mother made a clucking noise with her tongue. "Lord Aimery, I would not lie to you. My daughter indeed loves all those things, against the natural wont of women. But she is a good girl at heart, truly, and we, her parents, are to blame for any inappropriateness. As you know, she is our only living child, and hence Bartelmy's heir. My husband indulged her fancies because he wanted a boy so badly..."

"Don't blame *me*, Gerberga," said father, rather loudly, between gritted teeth. "You were no better..."

Mother did not look at him. "It can all be beaten out of her, if necessary. She can be wilful; I will admit that and, yes, perhaps I should have been sterner with her. Yet it seems her nature. Her nursemaids even have a nickname for her—Dangereuse."

"Dangereuse!" Aimery threw back his head and roared with laughter. "I like that! I prefer it to Amauberge. I shall call her that forever more."

"My Lord," I said, perplexed, "why should you call me anything?"

He grinned again, those blue eyes sparkling beneath dark brows. "Because, dear Dangereuse…I am going to marry you!"

And so it was done, as simple as that. If Aimery had been an old man, ugly and smelly, I might have shown my wilfulness and threatened to run away…or fled to the nearest nunnery, despite that I had called the nuns black crows. But I could not deny Aimery's attractiveness, and as a viscount, he was a good match indeed. My family were not poor but they did not move with the upper echelons either, and without a son to inherit, they depended on me and my future husband.

The wedding feast took place a week after my first meeting with Aimery. Father was determined the viscount would not have time to change his mind—as if he would! I could tell he was besotted with me. I had seen the look on other men's faces as I walked by, admiring and sometimes outright lustful. His expression held a sliver of both, although he kept the lust respectfully in check. That would come later, after the ceremony and the feast. I shivered at the thought, nervous but also full of strange anticipation. I was not ignorant like some maidens or like nuns given to God at an early age; I was ever curious about many things and had watched beasts in the fields with fascination, and once I had spied one of my sire's soldiers humping a washerwoman down by the river. Oh, how they had flopped and rolled and grappled in the shallows. I was unable to tear my half-horrified, half-amused gaze from their heaving and bucking, and no one dragged me away, for Betrana had succumbed to gripings in the gut and was relieving herself behind a tree. At first, the washerwoman's shrieks had made me think he was hurting her...but soon it became obvious they were cries of pleasure instead.

I hoped I would find 'the act' pleasurable myself, although it had certainly looked very undignified and silly. Some of the local women whispered a man's embrace was something to merely be endured but others giggled and blushed and sent each other sly, knowing looks. I knew I was beautiful, even though some said red hair was unlucky because Judas had red hair, so I presumed Aimery would treat me well, with tenderness and desire, more so than if he had wed an ugly lord's daughter just to get hold of her lands.

The wedding was held before the door of the village church so that there were many witnesses...and the castle chapel was considered too small and dingy anyway. There was greenery and flowers plaited together and hung over the doorframe with its Romanesque arch pecked with hideous gurning faces. The villagers came to gawk and marvel as I arrived in my sky-blue dress (the same one Aimery had seen me in—I had a few other gowns but it was by far my finest), pure as the Blessed Virgin herself, but with my long, unbound hair burning bright in the sunlight, twined with silver wires and topped by a chaplet—more Jezebel than Mary. A shame I would need to cover it before all men save Aimery from that day forward, but mother said some sacrifices had to be made.

Afterwards, the wedding party returned to the castle in high spirits. The nuptial feast was held in the Great Hall, where the servants had been hard at work all the previous day scrubbing, dusting and removing old reeds from the floor. Many pigs and dozens of chickens had been slaughtered, their meat served in trenchers of hard brown bread. Rare spices were sprinkled on top, costing my father more than he would ever admit. A variety of round cheeses glowed like yellow moons and for those with a sweet tooth, bronze platters brimmed with honey-sweetened oat cakes. Ale and wine flowed freely, emptying the stores in the castle vaults, which caused father some pain by the look on his face when he was told by the quivering steward.

When the final courses had been served, Betrana and my mother's two maids led me to the prepared bedchamber—my father's own, given to Aimery and me in honour of our union. The women smoothed out the sheets, lit the candles and hung pomanders around the chamber to freshen the air. Cheese, wine and grapes were brought in, should we wish to feast later in the night.

But I suspected, with thundering heart, that the only feasting would be upon each other.

The maids unlaced my gown and it foamed to the floor. My kirtle went next. The cool air hit my skin, made hairs rise on my arms and neck. Betrana began to sniffle. "I cannot believe you're all grown and wed. I remember when you were but a tiny babe…"

"Oh, Betrana, none of that," I said, glancing away before my own eyes grew wet.

I motioned to the other maids and they led me to the bed and tucked me between the sheets, artfully arranging the hair over my body like one of Salome's veils. I liked that thought—Salome, a dangerous temptress; my toes curled under the coverlet.

Outside the sturdy oak door of the bedchamber, I could hear the sounds of singing and carousing—Aimery and his knights, full of merriment and deep in their cups. I blushed at some of the bawdy things they roared, but not too much. I'd overheard soldiers on the gates say such things before.

Into the chamber they all piled, staggering and swaying, faces flushed, lips wet with wine. Aimery pulled ahead of them and looked at me, and the candle flames shimmering on the surfaces of his eyes, and the redness of his wine-wet lips sent a delicious shudder through me, a wave of heat that struck down like lightning into my loins. A wicked desire filled me to leap up and dance like Salome to the tune of the piper who accompanied my new husband. But I was not so bold; my thoughts were often improper but my actions a little more restrained.

Betrana and the maids now curtseyed and filed from the room. One of Aimery's companions, a strapping young fellow I heard Aimery call Ralph, pinched Betrana's bottom as she walked past. She grabbed the offended buttock with an outraged shriek then fled the chamber in high dudgeon.

The young men all roared with laughter, slapping each other's shoulders. Aimery, however, continued to gaze intently in my direction. "Enough merriment, fellows!" he said. "Get me ready for my bride!"

Another roar of mirth went up. I could see the drunken men sending covert gazes, or sometimes not so covert, in my direction as they dragged off Aimery's tunic and shirt and then his woollen drawers. I thought of what I had the urge to do earlier and burst into most unmaidenly laughter, which made the young knights laugh even harder themselves.

Aimery's leathern shoes were yanked off last and thrown across the room by the boisterous youths. My husband then pointed to the door. "Go! And if I suspect any of you are listening in, I will come and personally beat you black and blue!"

Staggering, the drunken revellers bashed their way out of the room, upsetting a jug of wine that ran across the floor.

Aimery scowled and looked about for a rag to wipe it up.

"Leave it," I commanded, "let the servants clean it in the morn. Come to bed...husband..."

He glanced from the wasted wine to me, sitting up in the bed, the covers drawn up. As he stared, I let the cover fall and climbed up onto my knees, my hair falling about me in a cloud. I put my hands beneath its flow and then thrust the heavy locks behind my white, smooth shoulders. Candlelight rippled across my nakedness.

"You...you are indeed well named Dangereuse!" Aimery breathed, "Not even a saint could resist, I'd wager!" and he dived toward the bed, the wind made by his rush extinguishing the glowing candles...

CHAPTER TWO

I was at my lord's castle in Châtellerault, his new wedded wife and mistress of his household. The castle, built over a hundred years ago by Aimery's ancestor, Viscount Airaud, was larger and finer than my parents' small holding, which was truly more of a fortified house than a castle strong enough for war. Here, there was a tall keep and an imposing curtain wall, a massive hall with a timber roof and wooden walkways to access the towers. I liked to walk the walls, peering out across the landscape below. Châtellerault was set in a fair location, the crossroads of four different counties—Poitou and Lorrain, Anjou and Berry. The Vienne River flowed along the fringes of the adjacent town, deep and swift, mirroring the sky, and beyond the southern town gate stood an immense dark forest, where my husband enjoyed the hunt, chasing swift, dappled deer and the grunting, tusked wild boar.

I swiftly learned, though, that my new life would not be one solely given to dancing, drinking and love-making. I had to grow up fast, learning all of what a chatelaine must know in order to look after her lord's holdings when he was away on business or in battle. Sadly, at first, some of the household staff seemed suspicious of me, whispering behind their hands about my nickname Dangereuse, which made me more determined than ever to use it all the time. I was given two maids to attend me, Eustachie and Pontia, a pair of sullen and suspicious girls. I hoped they would grow accustomed to me in time, but if not—to hell with them! I was their superior by right of my marriage and I was not there to make friends.

The town had a large market where I spent much time buying goods when Aimery was off on a hunt. He hunted frequently, which I found irritating, as he had no intention of taking me, despite my skill with hounds and horses. He laughed when I professed a desire to come along. "It would hardly suit you, all that blood!" he said, shaking his head. "And I'd look foolish before the men."

Jesu, so unfair, but such is the difference between men and women, and I could not force his hand. So on hot days, in his absence, I would take the languid maids down to the river's edge, where we would watch the boats and eat pastries and grapes from the market before returning home. Sometimes I would visit the great churches of Châtellerault, such as that of St Jacques, praying that my lord would come safely home without getting a boar's tusk thrust in his gut.

In perfect honesty, I was a little bored. Domesticity did not suit me in the way it suited most women, and Aimery, after an impassioned beginning to our marriage, began to fall in with unsavoury friends who treated their women like broodmares and who were crass and ill-mannered. I did not fear Aimery swiving other women—*pah*! Let him rut with such inferior beings if that was his wish—but his companions were another story. Drinking, dining, farting, belching…sometimes their behaviour was most odious and I was expected to smile sweetly at them all when they returned to Châtellerault after their adventures. There would be strange men falling about the castle hall for days, hair and raiment stiff with blood, half drunk from wine, half from elation at the kills they'd made…

Fortunately, something soon happened to turn my thoughts away from all this roistering by my handsome if not exactly brilliant-minded husband.

I fell pregnant.

I do not know why it was a surprise when it happened, for we rutted like beasts of the forest whenever Aimery was home, but surprised I was nonetheless. I had grown up hearing stories about unfortunate wives unable to give their lord the heirs they wanted. My own mother was such a one, unfortunately; I was her only babe for many years and then, after long barrenness, she produced a small, sickly boy. Oh, how my sire had rejoiced and I had felt forgotten…but then my brother died in his cradle, and there was weeping and wailing and my own mother was unable to look at me, making me surmise that she wished I had died instead. But this evil, unhappy time was long in the past, and my parents had come to accept God's will in the matter, and, in truth, had given me better education and more freedom that most rich men's daughters.

Being with child, I was now almost a sacred object to Aimery. He hunted less and spent more time in my company, making sure I ate the best of meals and had imported fruit if I desired. Oranges from Spain, dates, figs, olives—whatever I wanted was mine. He showered me with jewels, too—a diadem, ancient styled, with hanging beads of amethyst; a girdle of silver wires bound around green stones; exotic armbands from eastern lands snaking up my wrists; ear-drops with pearls that some old swindler had told him once belonged to Helen of Troy.

"You are my Helen," he said, as he sat gazing at me with adoration.

His riotous companions were truly out in the cold now, I thought with a smug little smile as I caressed my growing belly.

"Helen of Troy? Truly?" I teased. He looked unusually earnest.

"Yes, the most beautiful woman in the world—and yet, in her own way she was cursed...and dangerous. All those brave Greek kings and warriors fighting and dying for her love..."

"I solemnly promise never to behave like Helen," I said. "I have more dignity than to stand on the battlements and flash my paps at your enemies!"

"W—what!" he stammered, taken aback.

I choked back laughter. Clearly, he had never actually read the tales of Troy. My parents, whatever else they lacked, were learned people and imparted that learning to me once it became obvious I would end up their only heir. Mother and the local nuns taught me to read; the nuns supplied prayer books and mother loaned me more interesting texts with tales about Greeks and Trojans, Amazons and Alexander the Great.

"Did you not know, Aimery? When Helen faced down her murderous husband, Menelaus, after she abandoned him for Paris, she cooled his wrath by tearing open her garments to the waist! He took one look and could not slay her, no matter her faithlessness. She must have had wonderful breasts, Aimery, to have that kind of effect on a hardened warrior like Menelaus. Apparently, there were even cups shaped into their perfection—can you imagine that!"

His visage had turned fire-red. "N-no, not really!" he blurted.

"Men and women were much freer in those bygone days," I said thoughtfully. "They did not hide their passions over much, as we Christians do...or their bodies, for that matter. A Roman poet wrote about Helen that she hunted with her brothers—'with naked breasts she carried weapons, they say, and did not blush...' Perhaps when the babe arrives, we can go hunting together…alone, without your friends…I can be your Helen…"

He sputtered some more. "Dangereuse, I beg you stop this wild talk. It's not fitting. You are going to give birth to my son soon!"

"Yes." I caressed my belly. "And he was not begotten the immaculate conception, was he?"

Aimery took a deep breath; I felt a lecture coming on. Ever since I became with child, he had slowly grown more like a father instead of a lover, stolid and dutiful…save where his noisy, irritating companions were concerned. "No earthly child is…but come, woman, is it not the time to cease this lewd jesting? You are going to be a mother!"

I sighed, annoyed by this new, prudish side of him. "Things will change, of that I am certain, but I am who I am. I will never fade away like some wraith. Hiding in the background, afraid some man might spy a lock of my hair or an ankle! It was *your* choice to marry me, after all, and you seemed pleased enough to do it. I had no say in the matter."

"But you wanted to?" A note of hurt and anger hung in his voice.

"Yes, I liked the look of you," I said with some sarcasm. "You might have been old and scarred or hairy and smelly…"

"Enough!" Embarrassed, he glanced away, flapping a hand as if to dismiss me. "I can only assume this peevishness is caused by your condition. Let us not fight."

"We are not fighting. I am not anyway. I was merely teasing, for you have grown over serious of late. But I shall say no more, for it displeases you."

He appeared relieved. Rising, he bent to gently kiss my brow. "That is what I want to hear, Dangereuse. I understand our life together seems strange to you, and we have not been wed long. But you must accept the time of frivolity is past; there shall be no more riding out, hawking and other such activities."

"But whatever will you do with your time?" I understood exactly what he meant and was inwardly furious but pretended stupidity instead.

Aimery missed the barb in my question. "I meant *you*, my dearest. In your condition, you must rest more. I have heard how you are always in the town when I'm away, or in the fields flying your favourite hawk. It is not safe…"

"Why? Do you think someone will snatch me away, carry me off to a far-flung castle?"

"It has happened many times before…and your beauty has become quite legendary. Some men can be beasts."

"Yes, that much is certain," I said coolly, rising, my back giving a little jab of pain owing to the baby's weight. "Well now that you have told me what my life will entail forevermore, I shall go and find some 'womanly arts' to perform…"

He smiled, pleased by my response whilst seemingly completely unaware of my manner. Why had I not seen how stupid he was before?

I flounced to the door, pausing before I stepped into the corridor beyond.

"Womanly arts that might involve stabbing someone with my sewing needle!"

I gave birth to a boy that Aimery named Hugh after one of his long-dead ancestors. He was a large, lusty babe with dark red hair and a deep yell. We brought in a plump wetnurse from the local village to feed him, healthy, young and of good character—her baby was called Jacques and would have the honour of being Hugh's milk-brother.

Hugh's birth, which had been mercifully uncomplicated, restored Aimery to my bed, but not for long. He wanted another son as soon as possible, to ensure his patrimony would pass on. Children were, after all, horribly fragile and inclined to die young. I despised him for saying so to me, his face mournful; the idea of anything happening to Hugh was so horrible that I could not bear to countenance it, even though he was correct.

In any event, within months I was pregnant again and Aimery was glad and gave me a ruby on a gold chain, and then went back to his own pleasures and devices while I stayed cooped in the castle with my sulky maids, Eustachie and Pontia.

I began amusing myself by indulging in the purchase of expensive books on subjects my husband would not approve of. And I discovered the delights of troubadours and their art. A wandering minstrel on his way to Poitou stopped at Châtellerault, asking to sing for his supper and a pallet in the stable. He was an acolyte of Eble of Ventadorn, known as '*le chaunter*' and he regaled me, Pontia and Eustachie with songs of star-crossed lovers, secret trysts and other such folly. His name was Boso, and he was pleasant-faced and well-dressed, if a little faded, with a mane of brown curls falling across his brow in a rakish fashion. He tried to slip his hand to my posterior once, after reciting one of his more risqué poems; I slapped it sharply away and he blushed and set his attentions on the rapt Pontia instead. Later that very day I stumbled on them occupying a stall in the stables with articles of clothing and strands of hay flying. The horses looked terribly frightened, their eyes rolling at the hubbub. It was no concern of mine who Pontia slept with…but I sent Boso packing nonetheless. Too much distraction, and besides, Pontia was betrothed. I did not want bloodshed, and her intended was a minor knight with a bad temper, a jealous nature and a large axe!

In the winter, I birthed my second babe, but this time it was a girl. I asked permission to name her and it was granted. I chose the name Amable, hoping she would have a sweet nature. She had my looks but her hair was dark like her father's.

Aimery was at first disappointed that the baby was a girl, but then rubbed his chin and began to consider prospective matches for her. "I wonder," he said, rubbing his chin thoughtfully, "if she has your beauty when she's grown, how high a marriage we could make for her? The Duke of Aquitaine has sons…"

"She is but an infant; do not dare suggest she be contracted to some well-titled oaf and sent away at a young age," I said. "She stays here till she is at least twelve summers, do you understand, husband?"

He threw up his hands. "Yes, yes, but one needs to start early with these matters. You must learn to stop worrying your pretty head about them."

"Pah, better I overload my head than have a wholly empty skull…like some." I folded my arms, eyes narrowed.

He did not realise he was the target of my jibe. "Soon you will not have to worry about Amable so much. We will have more children…many more. You cannot have a special attachment to one, especially to a girl who will eventually be sent to her husband's household. You were lucky, Dangereuse—your father's stronghold is not so far away that you cannot, on occasion, visit, when I permit it. Many brides never see their birth families again."

"Thank you for reminding me, Aimery," I huffed, burning with indignation. I had only seen my family once since my marriage; Aimery made excuses whenever I asked. My mother had not even seen her grandchildren.

"I heard about that…that troubadour, by the way," Aimery continued, waggling his finger in my face like an old woman. "The one who tupped Pontia. Little trollop! She is lucky I do not tell Fulco, her betrothed. I forbid you to have such men in the castle when I am not here."

I snorted. "Not even if William, Duke of Aquitaine came here? Would you have me turn your overlord away? I have heard he is a great troubadour."

"*Especially* do not admit Duke William—even if you have to lie and fain plague or other sicknesses. He is my overlord, true enough, but I avoid him as much as I can. Cannot abide all that effete poetry. which he uses to charm almost every female he meets into bed…sometimes two at a time!"

"Interesting," I said. I had never before heard that.

"His first wife went to a convent because of his lechery, and I have heard the second is often away because she can barely stand to be around him…and he feels much the same about her."

William the troubadour sounded…*intriguing*. A man of sin, yet also of song. A heady brew.

"You must take me to Poitou at some time. I have never been."

"To meet William?" Aimery's lips curved in an angry sneer.

"No, because I have never seen it, and I've spent a lot of my time recently trapped within these four walls. Please do not make such a face, Aimery—my mother always told me that if I groaned and grimaced, my countenance might remain that way."

He looked surprised and then started to laugh; his mirth certainly made him appear more pleasant, more like the handsome young lord I had wed. "Ah, Dangereuse, you are incorrigible, but I would not have you any other way."

I wondered if he truly meant that as he wandered away into the castle's corridor, my presence forgotten, his attentions turned to more masculine pursuits. Before dawn's light touched the sky, he went out hunting with his brave fellows, their horns and yammering hounds waking up all and sundry within the castle.

I was left to the ponderous boredom of domesticity, as ever. Thoroughly annoyed, I put aside the little gown I was embroidering for Amable, and began to work on a tapestry depicting a bloody battle, my needle stabbing the knights over and over and over again....

I was soon with child once more; it seemed my husband's intention was that I should give him one child a year. Although, yes, yes, God was good, the harvest bounteous and all that—but birthing was a dangerous time for all women, even strong ones, and the long months of pregnancy worrisome and uncomfortable. So far, the births had all gone smoothly and had been surprisingly swift and easy, but I was well aware of the number of women who died in childbed or were never the same again afterwards, some left barren, others ailing with multiple complaints.

This time, I bore the much-desired second boy, a brother for little Hugh that we named Raoul. He was also loud and lusty, but dark-haired and green-eyed, with longer, less robust limbs than Hugh, although he seemed equally strong.

Aimery was pleased and a pearl headdress arrived and a brooch of fine gold which held at its heart a little fragment of the True Cross. Well, that's what Aimery believed anyway. I knew full well that they were so many wood chips out there purporting to be part of the True Cross that one could make a veritable forest out of them.

Months crawled by in Châtellerault, with Aimery coming and going as he pleased, while I—as I half-expected—was growing round with yet another babe.

"What if it is another girl?" Aimery groaned, less pleased than he had been in the past. His finances had suffered recently—too much expenditure on feasting his friends, buying new horses and augmenting his voluminous wardrobe. I knew the situation—I, after all, was left to the running of the household and oversaw the accounts—and viewed the empty coffers. Lately, he would order supplies of ale over staples like cheese and bread—I made sure his scrawls were erased and the items of greater necessity purchased.

"What if it is?" I said breezily. "You wanted lots of children—sons for heirs and for stalwart supporters and girls to make alliances with your neighbours so they won't try to burn the place to the ground…hopefully."

"True, true, I did think that once." He pulled a mournful, hangdog face. "But…but girls come with cost—their dowries, Dangereuse. How ever shall I pay for more than one or two? They'll have to become nuns."

I tapped my foot impatiently on the floor. "No…no nuns…unless the girl has a true calling. Abbesses want noble maiden's dowries too, you know. Brides of Christ need dower just like brides of men, it would seem.

But…you are getting too wound up by these thoughts; this next child is just as likely to be another boy."

But it was not a boy. Nor was it one girl but, to everyone's surprise, *two*. And both were born alive. Aimery was beside himself, although I could not tell whether with joy or with despair. My labour, this time, was hard, and afterwards, I waxed sore ill and thought that my life might be despaired of. It hung in the balance for the babes too, for it was seldom that two arrived together into this life and survived, but God shielded our family, for in the end both children lived and so did I. The girls were named Aenor and Aois.

It took me some time after their birth to feel well and strong again. Seeing me lying abed, bloodless and wan, weak as a newborn kitten, had scared Aimery—he left my bed wholly untouched now. This was a relief while I healed from my ordeal, but not ideal once I was well again. I was still young and had no wish to spend the rest of my days as chaste as a cloistered nun. There were forbidden ways to halt further conception and I was willing to use them.

Almery seemed less keen. I did not think his lack of interest was from any sudden piousness on his part and wondered if he had another woman on the side, or if, with five small children in the nursery, he saw me mostly as a 'mother' and not so much a wife…

Eventually, I put my foot down. We would have some truck with each other, even if not carnal. People were starting to talk.

"Aimery, it would seem our family is now complete," I said sweetly. "Surely it is time we did more together than occasionally rut if that is the case. I would like to see beyond Châtellerault. Take me to a great town…take me to Poitiers."

Aimery looked flustered. "But why?"

"Because that is what I desire." My nostrils flared as my eyes darkened with ill-suppressed annoyance. "I have given you what you want and need, have I not? Surely it is time for me to have something in return."

"You are a hard woman, Amauberge."

My lips compressed. As the passion between us ebbed away, he had started calling me by my birth name again. I did not like it, never had; its very sound made me feel as if I had become a dried-up old woman overnight.

"If you will not take me to Poitiers, I…I shall find a way to go by myself!" I cried, realising I sounded foolish but determined to impress upon him how desperate I was for some small glimmer of freedom.

Perplexed, he stared at me. "Well then…as you wish. We will go together. But I do not pretend to understand."

CHAPTER THREE

The sun was a bright golden coin in an azure sky the day we reached Poitiers. I had refused to ride in a litter or chariot, so arrived astride my white courser, Winter. My heart leapt at the sight of unfamiliar walls, ancient defences, that gleamed pale in the sunlight. Here Charles Martel had defeated the Paynim hordes; here saints had trodden and ancient kings with outlandish names ruled over courts wreathed in splendour.

We passed through one louring gateway, riding slowly through narrow streets full of timbered buildings. Ahead, through the crowds, I could see the gatehouse of a great fortified palace, with banners flapping above a sturdy donjon.

"That is Count William's Palace," said Aimery dully. "I supposed I shall have to see him. He will certainly know *I* am here."

Ah, the intriguing William. I smiled to myself, wondering if I might have the opportunity to meet him.

Our entourage proceeded to one of the great rich men's manses in the city, not far from the palace, where Aimery had arranged lodgings. We settled in, dining together in a stone hall full of candlelight, with woven hangings about the walls and fresh green rushes on the floor. That night, in the sweltering evening, with scents from the town and the flowers in the garden rising in a disconcerting mixture of foul and fair, I sought Aimery in his chamber. Although I did not particularly want to risk another child after the twins, and my husband had baulked at illicit means of prevention, I wanted all to be made right between us. And the high-quality wine had made me amorous.

But Aimery was not in the least interested. Chewing his fingernail in anxiety, he was pacing the floor of the bedchamber. Outside, the moon hung like a nail paring above a dark line of trees. In the distance, over the walls of the mansion house, I saw the faint ghostly heads of the towers of William's palace, pallid in the darkness.

"What is wrong, Aimery?" I asked, desire leeching out of me. I wrapped a shawl around my shoulders, hiding the flimsy kirtle I was wearing underneath.

"He knows I am here. William. He has summoned me into his presence tomorrow."

"It cannot be that bad, surely."

"He's my liege lord," said Aimery sulkily. He stopped chewing and folded his arms, sullen. "He will undoubtedly want something from me."

"Maybe I should come along…lighten the mood, befriend his wife."

"No!" Aimery's voice rose in a roar. Wild-eyed, he stared at me as if I had gone mad, although he, in that instant, was the one who looked truly insane. "Duke William is the last man a lady of quality should ever meet, I assure you."

I pursed my lips. "Ah, yes, you told me he has eyes for almost every woman he meets—save his unfortunate wife. Alas. I would have quite enjoyed listening to some of his poems, as well as those of the other troubadours and goliards who cluster around his court."

"You can find better things to do with your time than indulge in that nonsense," scowled Aimery. "There are three fine churches in Poitiers. Your time would be better spent there."

"Yes, always on my knees," I sighed, rolling my eyes. "In prayer." It was clear he would not be moved in the matter of visiting Duke William's court. "Oh well. I wish you goodnight then, Lord husband."

I left Aimery to stew on his forthcoming meeting and went out to cool my sticky flesh—and my temper—in the garden. As I strolled by the fishponds, lit by the moon, the stars bursting over the surface like white roses, I heard a voice rise in song somewhere out in the streets:

> *"From the place I adore,*
> *comes neither messenger nor missive;*
> *because of this, I sleep not, nor laugh;*
> *and I dare not come forward,*
> *until I know with certainty*
> *whether things stand as I want them to."*

I sighed. Things definitely did *not* stand as I wanted them to. Would they ever? As I contemplated, a mosquito dived onto my neck and nipped me. I swatted the creature dead, discarding its remains with a sweep of my hand. *Poor thing*...at least it had desired to kiss my throat, unlike my unwilling husband.

Aimery set off early to present himself to Duke William. I lay abed awhile, my two maids snoring on their pallets by the door. After I had risen, I bathed in a tub furled in silks, and then was dressed by Eustachie in a demure but rich gown of midnight blue. I wore a long white veil, banded beneath the chin.

Dangereuse was going out on the town.

I had wanted to travel on foot, but Pontia and Eustachie squealed that their shoes might get ruined and men might stare at them or grope at them if they were so openly displayed. Eustachie had grown excessively round in girth so I did not imagine much staring would take place, and Pontia…well, we all knew from her exploits with the troubadour Boso that she did not mind overmuch who saw what. Nevertheless, I gave in to the protests and hence we rode in a canopied litter over the bumpy cobblestones with a handful of armed men to keep the over-curious away.

Our first perambulations took us to the Hypogeum of the Dunes, where early Merovingian kings lay buried around a primitive altar in a crypt far underground, and to the huge table-rock, the Pierre Levee, where the locals held the fair of St Luke every year. It was said the rock was haunted by Faes who danced on the full moon nights and who sometimes captured human women to carry off. I wondered if Aimery would miss me if one of the Lordly People abducted me. If such beings existed, of course.

Then it was on to the shrine of St Radegund, Thuringian princess, Frankish Queen, who founded the Abbey of the Holy Cross in Poitiers, becoming a healer there. She was a true ascetic, eating no flesh, drinking no wine, and her wrists and neck were bound in iron circlets that cut into her flesh. I cannot imagine the pain, but perhaps it was less than when she had been one of five concubines taken by the war-like King Clotaire.

Radegund's church was a building in progress after the devastation of a great fire, its frontage covered in wooden scaffolding with masons chipping and hewing as they worked on dizzying heights. Leaving the litter, I headed inside to pay my respect to her bones, the maids trailing languidly after. Radegund was buried in the crypt below the church, her tomb capped with dark, worn stone, curled patterns decorating the stony pillow on which it lay. The walls dripped moisture, turning green, and the candles flickering in small, ancient archways made eerie shadows. Placing a gift of a gold coin on the shrine, I knelt in silent supplication. *Saint Radegund, you probably see me only as a lowly sinner, but you too were in a marriage chosen for you, and while mine is considerably better than yours, still it is no longer a happy one. Give me strength, Radegonde...and guide me, though not into your holy but oh so strict ways. Amen...*

It was not much of a prayer but then I was not truly the praying type, although I fulfilled my obligations to the church, attending mass, visiting shrines, doling out food to the poor and sick of Châtellerault...

I continued onward from St Radegund's church to the Baptistry of St John, one of Poitou's oldest buildings—indeed, some claimed the oldest Christian building in the West. Built on Roman foundations, it was a strange place where past strove against present; a baptismal font set in austere stone stood over a former pool for complete immersion. Murals were painted on several walls, jewel-like in hue—the Ascencion, the Evangelists, the Roman Emperor Constantine. Most whimsical was a scaly dragon which appeared to be begging a knight for its life. I almost pitied the poor thing. Knights! Always doing what they wished to poor dragons...or poor hapless maidens...

Leaving the Baptistry, I fared to the centre of town and the church of Saint Mary, not long completed, the west front a colourful panoply of figures from the Bible—Adam and Eve, King Nebuchadnezzar, King David and the Jesse Tree, Jacob battling the Angel. Over all of them, Christ stood within a nimbus, joined by the Sun and Moon and attended by flying Cherubim.

By this time, I was rather footsore and hungry and had partaken enough of the sanctified air of churches. My holiness was over for the day. I was more interested in eating…and in the palace next to the church, which was home to the elusive and intriguing William the Troubadour Duke—and where my husband was performing his feudal duties.

I retired to the litter with Eustachie and Pontia and sent a serving boy to go to the market stalls and bring purchase some food of decent quality. I promised him a beating if he brought back anything that might turn our bellies and send us running to the privy. He soon returned, puffing, carrying a selection of *pescods*, rissoles and hot sheep's feet flavoured with mustard, and some decent freshly baked bread to go with it.

I ate with my maids, peering out through the litter's draperies at the closed gates of Duke William's Palace. I could see nothing but an array of guardsmen, the sunlight glinting off their polished, pointed helms and a series of huge flapping banners emblazoned with William's emblem, a black eagle with outstretched wings.

I sighed, wiping my greasy fingers on a linen napkin proffered by Pontia. What did I expect? No doubt William and Aimery were locked deep within the palace, thrashing out some deal or other that would lose my husband some coin and increase William's coffers. They were hardly going to appear in an eye's blink and ride out of the palace.

But then…they did exactly that. A trumpet shouted, its deep, brazen voice ringing out over the market square, followed by another and then another. All the hucksters, bakers, fishmongers and butchers halted their activities, as did the busy housewives, cowled nuns, fat merchants and even-fatter monks with their dusty sandalled feet. Even the handless beggar crouched on the corner stopped his constant yowls for alms. All eyes turned towards the palace.

The huge front gate was grinding open, the sound harsh and deafening; the space behind it filled with brightly caparisoned horses, champing and straining to be free. "Oh, my lady Dangereuse!" breathed Eustachie, her eyes as round as her belly, crumbs from her meal dappling her plump chin. "What if Lord Aimery see us?"

The maid was right; to be caught by my husband peering in would be a Very Bad Thing. If I had merely been seen emerging from the nearby church, pious meek and carefully veiled, perhaps I would get away with it. But if I was caught lurking in the market square like some fishwife (or worse), with the gnawed remains of my dinner on a bread trencher, and my hair hanging down after I had discarded my wimple in the heat, it would look as if I had settled in to spy on my husband—which was indeed what I was doing, though inadvertently. But it was not Aimery I was interested in seeing but rather the infamous and flamboyant William.

"Quick, quick!" I beckoned frantically to my guards. "Get this litter out of the way of Duke William's men. To the back…behind the crowds."

The men, alarmed by both my vehemence and my wildly flapping arm, raced to obey my command. Jolting and jarring, the litter was dragged over the bumpy cobblestones. My trencher tipped over; splotches of mustard yellowed my fine pillows. Eustachie squawked and fell over at one severe jolt. A half-filled carafe of wine jiggled; as Pontia grabbed it, the contents splashed up and reddened the front of her gown, making it look as if she had been stabbed. On all sides, townsfolk snarled and cursed at us for pushing through their ranks; they looked decidedly unfriendly, so I motioned for the men, who were also losing their tempers and reaching for their weapons, to place the litter down behind a relic seller's stand, out of the way— and out of eyesight should Aimery or William go by. Then I told the maids to get out and mingle with the crowd; obediently they struggled out of the litter and plunged into the milling throng. I flung my wimple back on, crooked but at least some cover, and hurried after them, watching them stop against the church's west front where they huddled beneath a looming toothy gargoyle.

I considered joining them but now that I was out of the litter, my curiosity drew me forward. I was less noticeable now, mingling with the crowd. It was foolhardy, even dangerous, but I felt drawn forward as if I were a puppet on the string. Or maybe it was Mistress Fate, urging me on…or even a minor imp whispering in my ear.

I pushed back towards the front of the onlookers, standing behind a burly old woman in a weathered brown homespun dress and peering over her shoulder, which was quite easy, for I am taller than most women.

Onwards came the Duke's entourage, horses' hoofs clattering on the cobbles, banners flaring. I spotted Aimery and pulled up a fold of my veil to cover the lower half of my face. He was not glancing in my direction anyway; he rode at Duke William's side, shoulders slightly hunched, face showing what I knew to be displeasure rather than the solemnity required on a dignified occasion. Next to him, William was like the sun battling against the night. He was maybe an inch or two shorter, as far as I could tell, but far more muscular, his thick wavy hair a shade of brown touched by flame, a startling deep russet like an autumn leaf. He had a cheerful countenance as he waved with a richly gloved hand to those who thronged the streets.

The woman in front of me began to yawp excitedly and flail her arms, hurling a small bouquet beneath the hoofs of the Duke's oncoming steed. The flying flowers made the beast fret and pull hard on its bit, and William glanced over...straight in my direction.

His gazes skimmed the peasant woman who had thrown the posy...and landed on me. Our eyes met. My heart began to hammer and my ears rang. My hands fell limply to my side, loosing the veil I had drawn up for secrecy. My whole face revealed, I stepped out from behind the old woman. I did not even care that Aimery might see me, but as it happened, he was staring in the opposite direction, lost in his own thoughts.

Duke William's full lips drew up in a smile and he nodded in my direction, an almost indiscernible motion of his head. My cheeks burned like those of a gauche young maiden. Then he was gone in a flurry of pennants and horses, and feeling suddenly embarrassed and very exposed, I rushed back to find my maids and the litter.

I hurried back to the manse, fearing the worst—that Aimery would have brought the Duke hither to continue some kind of negotiations, but thankfully I found our lodgings at peace, the servants busy with their daily toil. Without delay, I went to my chamber and changed my garments just in case Aimery might have spied me in the crowd. I would deny all, insist it was merely a trick of his imagination.

My husband returned shortly after dusk, when moths and other insects were battering around the torches bracketed above the entrance door as if seeking to immolate themselves in the flames. As he entered the hall where I waited, the dutiful wife, he looked gloomy, his mouth in a sour pout. The scent of wine clung to him.

"How was your visit with the Duke?" I asked with mock cheerfulness. "You smell like you've had a good time."

He grunted and flung himself down on a bench. "The wine he gave me was the only thing that made the day bearable. He dragged me all around the town defences…showing me the weak parts, which he expects me to help rebuild."

"That is part of your duties, surely."

Aimery shot me a withering glare. "Yes, but I'd rather such obligations had not come at this very moment. My treasury is depleted, as you know, Dangereuse. The crops have been poor. I'm late collecting the rents. And it is not merely repairs in Poitiers for which William demands contributions—he wants to come hunting or fishing on our lands whenever he pleases."

My heartbeat quickened. I turned away, toward the central fire, afraid my excitement would be all too visible on my face. "Oh?"

"His right of course—*droit de garenne*. But it galls me to think he will take the pleasure of the hunt away from me as well as my meagre coin."

"I am sure he will not cripple you financially—it's not in his best interests to do so. And the Duke taking one or two little boars or stags from the forest won't hurt us either. At any rate…" I shrugged. "It has to be done; there is no point in endless complaints."

"Yes, I *know* that," he snapped, in high dudgeon. He ripped off his riding gloves, flung them on a table. "We go home tomorrow, and hope to Hell the Duke forgets much of what was spoken today! With all his troubadour friends marching about his castle, yowling like cats with trodden on tails, I am surprised the man can even think straight!"

He stalked out of the room, trailing gloom. I smiled secretly to myself as I watched him depart. Aimery did not want Duke William to visit Châtellerault—but having seen him in the market square, I certainly did.

CHAPTER FOUR

In the Autumn of that year, when the trees were turned as gold as a king's mantle, as red as the crimson blood spilt on a battlefield, William of Aquitaine sent a message to Aimery. Within a week, he would arrive with his entourage and expected food and accommodation for each and every member of his party, as well as several hunting trips in the game-filled woodlands.

Aimery was in a foul mood at the thought, pacing around our castle and kicking out at the ever-scavenging dogs in the hall.

"Do not do that, husband," I chided him as one of the hounds narrowly avoided his boot and scurried under a table. "It is not the dogs' fault. Now, help me to instruct the servants to prepare for our noble guest. Is William bringing his wife, Duchess Philippa?"

Aimery slunk to the empty high seat on the dais and flopped into it. "No, I believe not. She's still away in Toulouse. It is not a happy match, complicated by their son, William, who resides with his father, as is correct, but who supports his mother in all things. He fights with his sire whenever they are in the same room; I witnessed a few of his tantrums when we were in Poitiers. I pray the brat is not coming."

But the brat did, along with his father. On a sunny golden late September afternoon, with woodsmoke curling in the air and the promise of coming winter in the wind, William and his heir rode up to the castle gates with their entourage.

Dressed in his best gown and cloak, Aimery went out to greet them; from my bedchamber's slit window, I peered down as the two men gave each other the kiss of peace. Aimery then moved to William's son, who was standing near his father, a very tall, broad boy who barely resembled his sire and who looked as miserable as sin. His arms were folded impudently over his radiant saffron-hued tunic; I thought he probably needed a few beatings to cure him of his ill-manners and guessed he was most certainly a mother's boy. Eventually, he dropped his arms and made a curt bow to Aimery, his whole frame oozing disdain.

I moved away from the window. Pontia was sewing, while Eustachie was polishing off the last of a plate of sweetmeats, her fingers sticky with honey. I clapped my hands loudly, making the two women jump. "Did you not hear the trumpets call? It is time to prepare for the banquet. The Duke of Aquitaine has arrived from Poitiers."

There was a flutter of gowns, threads and tapestries as the women left their positions and hurried to assist me. My day-robe was removed and a rich gown of a dark blueish-purple drawn over my kirtle. Long sleeves trimmed with gold tissue hung almost to the ground, and a girdle of meshed silver wires threaded with deep red gems like flashing eyes cinched my waist—which, thanks be to the Virgin, had not expanded overmuch despite the children I had borne. I was lucky that way; tall but of a slight, lean build with long slim legs, I suspected I would not run to matronly stoutness.

I wished I could wear my hair loose, but as a married woman that would be considered shocking and scandalous, and there was no way I could get away with it. However, I had Eustachie set a fetching circlet on it, with a sheer, iridescent veil tailing behind. My hair was braided decently and plaited with blue ribbons that set off the hot colour of it.

I admired myself in a polished brass plate, wishing the image was clearer. My face wobbled and warped on the metallic surface but I had to admit I still looked well, not at all like some portly mother of five.

"Bring me scent!" I ordered, and Pontia carried over a graceful glass bottle with shimmering, iridescent designs in rainbow colours. It was, apparently, a Roman relic brought back from a crusade and given into the keeping of Aimery's family. The perfume inside was from Moorish Spain and made from a blend of olive oil, cinnamon and myrrh. I snatched the bottle and daubed the lotion on my neck, on my wrists. The perfume wafted around me, sweet and heady.

Moving in a stately fashion, I left my apartments, the maids following in my wake. As I entered the Great Hall, I raised my chin and proceeded toward the dais and the high table with its starched linen covers. Aimery was talking to the Duke; at William's side slouched the sullen boy. To my horror, the steward was guiding me, not to my husband's side (or better yet, William's) but to that of young William—who, upon seeing his mulish pout, I had secretly decided to nickname 'Little Willy.' I was furious and perplexed as to why Aimery had allowed such a move— unless it was to keep me as far as possible from the troubadour lord. Fair enough, knowing William's reputation…but to sit me next to a spotty young lout whose outthrust lower lip looked like it might droop onto his trencher!

A woman of my position dared not make a fuss in public, so I sat down at my appointed place, schooling my face into calmness. From beneath lowered eyelashes, however, I could see the usual gossips whispering in each other's ears, evidently amused by my situation. Fury kindled in my heart and with great gusto, I grasped my eating knife and attacked the first course of the banquet as it landed on the table—and a speared green pickle flew off my knife's tip and landed in Little Willy's lap.

A gasp broke from his lips and both of us stared at the slimy trail on his silken tunic. I noticed his hands trembling and wondered if he would start shouting, but after a few seconds, he appeared to get hold of himself.

"I beg your pardon, young sir." I cast him my sweetest, most conciliatory smile. "An unfortunate accident."

My charms did not seem to work on him as they did on most men. He grunted something in a sulky tone and began to slurp on the cook's famous cabbage soup, with its seasonings of coriander, saffron and onions. What an irritating little coxcomb. He did not seem to care one jot that the soup was dappling his tunic now, joining the marks left from the unfortunate pickle.

I made an effort to ignore him, and continued supping on the delicacies set before me—fish mortrews; savoury pate made with almonds and ginger; venison stakes stewed in wine and the juice of Seville oranges; and when all else was done, rose pudding topped with cream and pine nuts.

Suddenly our household musicians, who had played soft, sweet melodies on lyre and dulcimer while we dined, ceased to play. I glanced up from my trencher at the unexpected silence. The steward was shepherding them out the door...and another company came in.

These were also musicians but they were most unlike our timid, languid fellows with their reedy pipes and quietly twanging harps. A company of men in bright hats and vivid garments redolent of exotic lands stood before the dais. They bore, shawm and sackbut, tabor and wheezing bagpipes, drums and horns carved from tusks and bound in silver. They were strangers to me, and as I doubted that Aimery would open his purse to hire such entertainers, I surmised they had travelled with Duke William as part of his retinue. My suspicions were proved correct when the Duke's retainers began to cheer and stamp their feet while the gathered minstrels belted out a loud, dramatic song. Of William's company, only petulant young Willy looked unenthused, rolling his eyes heavenward and sighing.

By the time the musicians finished their raucous number, almost everyone was out of their seats and cheering. I clapped brightly myself; never had our hall seemed so merry, so alive.

The minstrels bowed and moved to one side, and now one of the Duke's troubadours emerged, wearing outlandish poison-green robes and a massive domed hat with a crimson feather thrust into it. He placed a graceful hand on his breast and began to sing in a high-pitched tone of lost love, of longing, of the lady who owned his heart but belonged to another.

Most of those in the Hall were entranced, especially the ladies…but Aimery, passing my seat after a trip to the privy, muttered, "Christ, this caterwauling hurts my head!"

I ignored his comment and continued to listen to the troubadour. As soon as the man's final song dissolved into a furious wave of clapping, I rose, unpinned a brooch from my shoulder and threw it to him as a payment for his efforts. He caught it expertly and bowed so low the tail of his extraordinary hat swept the rushes. More cheering and hollering reverberated around the Great Hall, ringing to the rafters.

At that moment, all eyes were upon me and the troubadour. Aimery looked disgruntled, Little Willy sneering, but there was another in the room whose look was one of approval…and more besides.

Duke William was leaning back in his chair, wearing a satisfied smile. It was almost as if he had planned to impress me with his servant's talent all along. His gaze met mine, and our eyes locked, held; his sparkled, half in shadow from the flickering candles. Pools of deep wine, willing me to fall in, to drown.

Suddenly the whole room seemed to go quiet, but I realised, with a shock, that the silence was only in my head. The usual noise of feasting was going on, but it was as if I was caught within a strange, magical bubble, separate from the rest of the revellers—with William, Count of Poitou, Duke of Aquitaine.

I had never experienced such a sensation and heat flooded into my cheeks, making them burn. My body tingled head to toe and my breathing deepened. Tales spoke of female witches who ensnared men with their allure— were there male sorcerers who entranced hapless women in similar manner? Despite having five children, I felt as if I were a young girl again, my heart light and full of unknown longing…yet also, I was aware the innocence of maidenhood was long gone, and I understood what was running through my blood in a dark, hot stream.

Desire. Yearning. *Lust…*

Duke William leapt up, spry and swift. With one hand, he gestured to the musicians waiting on the sidelines and they pranced onto the floor again, beginning a violently merry tune.

"Now, it is time to dance!" the Duke cried over the din.

In three strides, he had reached my side. I swear Aimery's jaw nearly smote the floor, but he seemed stricken, bound with indecision, not knowing what move he might make to stop us meeting. William was his liege lord, after all—how could he forbid him a simple dance with his wife?

"My Lady Amauberge, will you dance with me?" William asked. He glanced aside at Aimery, feigning politeness, his eyes daring him to say no or make a scene.

My husband glowered, countenance threatening as a thunderhead, but he said nothing and grabbed furiously at his wine goblet.

I walked out into the centre of the Great Hall on the arm of the Duke. He smelt of sandalwood and horses, a heady mix. Around us, other couples joined in the dance. Aimery remained frowning at the high table, as did Little Willy.

William's arm touched my waist; it was as if a bolt of lightning ran through me. My head felt giddy. Leaning over, as the dancers massed in the centre of the hall and hid us from Aimery's gaze, he murmured in my ear, "I remember you from the Market Square. In my town of Poitiers."

My eyes widened. "Yes…yes, I was there…But how did you know who I was?"

He laughed, a deep, rich sound that rumbled in his chest and sent a warm thrill through me. "When I saw you, I immediately sent spies to track you down. You were not hard to find."

My brows lifted. "You went to great effort to track down a stranger from the Market Place."

"No, not in my estimation. A beautiful woman's worth is beyond the rubies of the world. She is always well worth...*tracking*."

"Overblown flattery, my lord Duke," I scoffed.

"Oh, no, I *do* mean it, Amauberge."

"Please, do not call me that name, sire. I am known as Dangereuse."

"A fitting name. I admit I had heard before today of the beauty and fire of my vassal's wife. A dangerous lady, they say. Seductive."

"Perhaps." I twirled away from him, sleeves and headdress flying; he caught my wrist and pulled me back, almost making me lose my balance.

"I did not come here for hunting as your dullard husband thinks," he said. "I came to see you...to persuade you to come away with me."

"You are mad," I replied, voice quaking. "You must have imbibed too much drink, my lord Duke."

"I can see in your eyes, you feel what I feel," he said. "I want you, Dangereuse. Of all the women I have bedded—and I will not lie, there have been many, you entrance me like...like Cleopatra entranced Caesar and Mark Anthony, like Jezebel and Ahab, Samson and Delilah..."

"Or maybe like Salome with her Dance, who ordered John the Baptist's head be given her on a platter." I offered a tight little smile.

"You surely would not want my head when all I want is to honour you, put you up on a pedestal above all earthly woman, shower you in rose petals and jewels....'"

"I am married. You are married. You would make a harlot of me."

"My wife is a shrew. She seldom stays at home. And I…I am no fool; I can see Aimery bores you. And that is no surprise—he is a boring man."

"Well, he can be, I speak with an honest heart here, but what you suggest is preposterous…monstrous, even."

"I will win you. I swear I will have you, even if I have to challenge Aimery to a duel for your love."

Fear now flooded through me; the giddiness in my head cleared, and any hint of flirtatiousness died, realising sudden dangers that swirled about me, threatening all I knew. If Duke William challenged Aimery and killed him in some kind of mad duel, my poor children would lose all…

"No, not that!" I cried, grasping his wrist.

My impassioned cry, perhaps the fright in my eyes, halted any further threats from the Duke. Indeed, he looked slightly dazed as if he, too, was shocked at what he had proposed. After all, his conquests were legendary—surely, I was no more than a momentary glimmer in his roving eye.

The music died with a wail. William escorted me back to my seat on the dais. Young Willy was glaring, his cheeks florid and his eyes almost bulging from their sockets. Aimery was also scowling, his brows lowered and drawn together.

As I went to sit, Willy sprang up as if he had been scalded and shouted at his father, "Why do you bring me along with you on these expeditions? Every time it is the same—you dishonour me and my mother by chasing after every whore you can lay hands on."

"Whore? How dare you insult my wife!" Aimery reacted, leaping up and kicking his bench over with a tremendous crash. "I'll teach you a lesson in manners, you foul-mouthed little whelp."

I stood between man and youth, glancing furiously from one to the other—and to Duke William, who had started this foolishness. "Enough!" I shouted above the din. "You are all behaving like fools. You are men, not beasts—so act like men!" I whirled about to young William. "And you...*child*. If I ever hear you call me such a name again, I will have you stripped naked and will birch your white arse in front of the entire garrison until you bleed!"

The boy gasped in outrage and grabbed at his eating dagger. Now Count William intervened, catching his son by the scruff of the neck and shaking him like a terrier shakes a rat.

"William!" he spat in his face. "Get you to the stables before I beat you in the very manner the Lady has described." He grabbed Little Willy's knife and gave him a strong push that sent him reeling across the room. Then he turned in my direction and bowed. "I apologise on William's behalf, Lady Dangereuse. And I apologise to you too, Aimery..." He nodded toward my beetle-browed husband. "I did not intend the evening to end this way."

No, I thought...*not this way...but you were hoping it would end in another, also wholly inappropriate way...*

"I will depart immediately with my company," continued the Duke. "It would be wrong to impose further on your hospitality."

"You...you do not have to leave," stammered my husband, all too aware that William was his liege lord, and it would do well to humour him, no matter what had happened.

But William had resolved to leave. Giving me another bow, he turned on his heel and marched from the Great Hall, Little Willy glowering at his heels, his demeanour that of a whipped cur, and his troubadours, musicians, knights and companions following after.

As soon as they left, it was as if my heart had been rent. What in God's Name wrong with me—had I been possessed? Pushing past Aimery, I plunged into the nearby corridor and ran for my bedchamber.

That night I dreamed…of William of Aquitaine. Of William riding away. And I was both angry and despairing all at once.

CHAPTER FIVE

A few months after the fiasco at Châtellerault, Duke William wrote to Aimery, offering reparations and promising to 'mend their friendship.' Aimery was duly relieved, for he had feared the Count would take offence and require greater and greater payments and services.

William even mentioned hunting in the forest again, but promised to bring no hangers-on that would need food and shelter—and certainly not his volatile young heir.

My heart began a swift beating when I heard the news. "When will you meet with him?" I asked, keeping my voice level. "It would be good to make certain no animosity lies between you."

"Next month," replied Aimery, crumpling up William's missive and tossing it on the hearth. "While I cannot say I am looking forward to it, it is true that our relationship must be made well."

I nodded and left him to plan the details of the hunt. My mind whirled. How could I meet William…alone? I knew I played a dangerous game, but I had set my heart on it and was determined to prove my name true. The past months had been a strange time—Aimery attentive then distant, my own manner loving then cold and confused. How had my husband once seemed so handsome? Now he had grown spare and too lean, almost gaunt, his face browned by the sun like that of the peasants in the fields. His hair had thinned and he scraped it back, which gave him a hawkish appearance. His mannerisms had grown worse, in turns miserly and dull. We spent little time together, and in my eyes, the castle had begun to look drab and unhomely. The children…yes, I spent time with them, laughed at their chatter, witnessed first footsteps and heard first halting words…but I had to admit, that while some women were natural mothers, I was not one of them. I was secretly glad when the nurses took them away and I could be free of crying, temper tantrums and the smell of swaddling and baby-sick.

I dreamed of troubadours, of dancing in candle-lit halls, of riding through the fields in the moonlight. Girlish fancies maybe, but I craved them. And more than that, I craved William, his aura of power, intelligence and humour…the strength of his arms, the press of his thighs.

Oh, how wicked I was.

The day of the hunt drew nearer. Aimery was fretting, eager to right things for once and for all. "I shall be away for a few nights," he told me. "There is a lodge within the forest where the hunting party shall stay. Therefore, you won't be disturbed in your daily routine by any unwanted guests."

Unwanted? If only he knew.

"I have been to the Lodge; do you not remember?" I asked. He certainly *should* remember. He had taken me there in the early days of our marriage, and our eldest son Hugh had been conceived within the old lodge with its moss-furred stone walls and ancient, time-warped beams.

"Oh, have you? I cannot recall such a visit," he said thoughtlessly, shaking his head. "Anyway, that is where I shall meet with Count William while we hunt. Wish me luck, dear wife; maybe I shall bring down a fine stag or boar for the table."

"Hmm." I stared at the floor to hide my expression. *Perhaps I would do some hunting of my own…*

The next few days were filled with indecision as the good wife Amauberge, mother of five, warred with the wicked, wanton Dangereuse de l'Isle Bouchard. I wandered to the castle chapel, prayed to have all sinfulness cleansed from my soul—but my wickedness remained, burning hot as all the flames of Hell, urging me onwards. The love I had once borne for my husband had withered on the vine…I wanted William the Troubadour lord. And I knew he wanted me. Or at least I hoped he still did. My hands grew sweaty with nerves and my stomach roiled at the thought he might have forgotten me and gone on to some other conquest he preferred…

Determined now to have my way, no matter how grave the sin, I sent a servant boy I trusted to the local inn to contact one of the couriers who went to and fro across Aquitaine bearing messages for money. I gave the lad a parchment, sealed with Aimery's own seal (carefully removed from his treasury on a midnight raid), but with a letter written by me inside. I told William that I knew he planned to hunt in the forest with my husband. *If you want to hunt down a fair white doe, of great rarity, that too can be arranged,* I wrote. *On the second day you are at the Lodge, do not retire for the Second Sleep but go to the little dell filled with fairy-like flowers and you will find your quarry grazing there…"*

My messenger boy ran out of the castle gates and down the town's street. I watched till he vanished into the crowds and then turned away. I had set my course now and dared not falter.

I might end up humiliated; maybe William would not show up to our secret assignation near the lodge. Maybe he would refuse to see me as a punishment for my initial rejection. If that happened, I would return to Châtellerault and take a vow to better myself and tend more to the womanly arts. I would give away my books, save for those on religion only, and bestow my silks and jewels on the poor.

But if William still desired me... I shuddered. Suddenly the castle walls around me seemed very like a prison, and I longed for nothing more to break free, though it should destroy my reputation forever...

Aimery left for the planned hunt, looking happier than I had seen him in a while. "Off to my rendezvous with the Duke!" he had said cheerily as he rode down the barbican. I had to curb a wicked smile. planned to rendezvous with him too, but Aimery would know none of *that*. It was a daring scheme, though, even as such illicit assignations went. I would have to get out of the castle unnoticed and ride away unseen as soon as the daylight failed. I could take no maid for company, nor anyone else, not even the messenger boy who had taken my letter to the courier, face glowing with delight as I placed several gold coins into his palm. I must ride the roads alone, facing any dangers that might haunt them, and the best way to do that safely would be to wear a man's garb.

On the pretext of inspecting a new wall hanging that had arrived, I went to Aimery's apartments and rummaged through his clothing chests. A loose dark tunic, a pair of wool drawers and long socks. A plain cloak with a deep hood. The shoes would have to stay behind; all far too big for my feet, making it difficult to run should I need to.

Draping the garments over my arm, I slipped back to my own quarters and donned them, tucking my hair in beneath the hood. Pontia and Eustachie had been given leave for the night and had vanished to visit family, or lovers, or whatever else they liked to do. They may have wondered about my sudden need for solitude but they had been taught never to question—and not to gossip outside the castle. Before they departed, I had clutched my belly, groaning piteously, implying that my monthly courses were bothering me, and being women, they knew well that misery.

As a final finishing touch to keep any nosy maid at bay, I shifted the bolster on the bed, bunched up the pillows into a vaguely human shape and crumpled up a thick coverlet over them. The result was rather unconvincing but I had told Portia and Eustachie I wanted no bother from anyone, on the pain of my displeasure, so I doubted they would do more than peep in…till they became concerned anyway

Then I waited, watching as the sun sank over the roofs of the town, red as blood. Night's mantle fell, followed by a mist that coiled up from the ground, forming yet another cloak of concealment. I did not know whether to feel happy or concerned—a heavy mist was good to hide in, but less good for safe travel to a destination I had never travelled alone to before, let alone unaccompanied in the darkness.

Outside the chamber, the halls began to fall silent. Someone whistled while going about their tasks in the bailey. I crept out of my room, moving furtively down the corridors and out into the gloom of the courtyard. Furled in shadow, hastily I slinked along the wall, making my way towards the postern gate, which led out onto marshy land bounded by the river. The postern was seldom guarded, for the swift, deep river formed a strong barrier against attack from that direction. The gateway was meant as an escape route should the front gates and inner bailey be breached…and it was, as the maids had told me, a frequent spot for lovers' meetings owing to its quietness. It was quite near the chutes from the privies, which made passion in the long grass seem rather improbable, but at any rate, I doubted I would find anyone there.

I had now reached the small garden, its herbs crushing beneath my rabbit skin boots and sending up an acrid though pleasant scent into the gloom. Ahead, I could see the vast, dark bulk of the wall with its fanged crenels hard against the sky. The outline of the postern gate became visible through the ground fog—wood crisscrossed with rusted iron struts. Reaching it, I gripped the huge oak bar that crossed its surface. Some women would not have had the strength to lift such a weight, but not only was I taller than woman's wont, I was also unusually strong. With a minimal amount of effort, I shifted the bar from its position and it dropped with a low thud into the nearby flowerbed.

Grasping the corroded door ring, I turned it and pushed the door open a mere crack. I held on to the ring, in case a gust of wind should rip the door from my hands and slam it against the wall, making an obvious noise that would bring sentries running. Peeking out, I saw no one in sight. The mist was coiling like spectres on the sluggish flow of the river. I smelt the reek of the waters…and the ever-present privies.

Wrinkling my nose in disgust, I hurried out of the postern, closing it quietly behind me and keeping close to the wall as I felt the wet earth sink and squish beneath my feet. A little bit further and there would be a dark thicket growing to the left of the nursery tower. That's where the lovers met, I presumed, rather than the stinking garderobe area…and it was also where my mount would be waiting.

As I drew nearer, thorny brambles catching at my cloak, I heard a horse's soft whicker and the stamp of hoofs. Rounding the bushes, I saw a little grey mare tied to a tree branch by a rope. I had sent a servant out to buy a gentle but sturdy animal from the horse market, using the lie that she would be a mount for one of the children. Once he had brought her home, I had ridden her around the castle grounds and parkland beyond for a while, 'testing her out', before guiding her down to the riverside, where I tethered her to a tree to await my later arrival.

Taking great care, I climbed into the saddle. The mare was a placid thing who did not appear to have a single spark of fire, but the seller claimed she had a good, strong heart and could move at a steady pace when required. I prayed he had not told falsehoods merely to make a sale and that the mare would not have a hard mouth unresponsive to the bit or go lame halfway through the journey.

Lightly I set my heels to the mare's flanks and to my surprise, she came to sudden life, dancing under my weight. It was as if she, too, was inflamed at the prospect of our momentous journey. "Do not fail me, my little steed!" I murmured in her soft ear, and together we cantered away from Châtellerault into the misty darkness.

The forest where the men hunted was not terribly far from the town of Châtellerault, but cloaked by the night and swathed in mist, the way thither almost resembled a mysterious and somewhat ominous otherworld. No wanderers fared abroad on the road—which was a small mercy—but such desolation was eerie too, with vapours rising like empty shrouds and the thickness of the fog deadening all sound. The fog had grown so thick that even the stars were blotted out and dampness seeped through my warm garments, making me shiver uncontrollably despite myself. I began to think of foolish old legends from my childhood—of corpse-candles bobbing in the fog, of night-hags and headless revenants riding the path to hell and taking unwary wanderers with them…

I pulled the reigns tight as the wind drifted the sound of singing and music to my ears, distorted by the fog. Fright gripped my heart as I recalled the tales of the palaces of the Fae, where the immortal folk caroused under earthen mounds, waiting to capture humans and force them to join their endless dance. But when morning came, there would be no blessed freedom for the captive—the unfortunate mortal would stagger forth from the Fae hillock to collapse into a pile of fleshless bones, for a hundred years would have gone past, a century lost in what seemed a single night…

Abruptly I shook my head, clearing it of such unwholesome fancies. Within the cavern of my hood, I grinned at my own folly. I was near my destination; the hunting lodge lay down a winding but well-marked path leading from the main road to a shallow treed gully—the sounds of revelry were not those made by malign Faes but rather drunken lords roistering within the lodge's walls. Above the noise of drinking men, a pipe wailed, a drum boomed, a troubadour sang a raucous ballad. Who else but Count William would have brought such entertainers with him on a hunt?

I pressed my heels to the mare's flanks again and slowly guided her off the road. The fog was rising a little and I could see the track a little more clearly. Even night-locked and mist-encased, there was a slight familiarity.

I was well on my way to the place of my sinful assignation; I shuddered at the thought. This was the great turning point of my life; I felt the hand of destiny upon my shoulder. Tonight, one of the several things would happen—I could end up Duke William's mistress, his discarded harlot after a solitary union, or perhaps even just remain Aimery's faithless-in-heart wife after being rejected untouched by her would-be paramour. One of these outcomes I desired greatly, another I would accept if I had to…but the last one would break my spirit—and—my heart forever.

I rode deeper into the woods. Droplets of moisture rolled from the trees, pattering on my horse's mane and on my shoulders and hood. Ahead, a golden light shone; a lantern, its rays diffused and made surreal by the mist. I knew that lantern; it hung from the gate built into the wooded palisade around the hunting lodge. I paused a moment, eyeing it, as it swung in the breeze. This was my final chance—did I go where my wild, dangerous heart desired? Or did I turn around and go home, choosing the path of quiet domesticity, where I would wither like a plucked rose behind the walls of Châtellerault, fading until there was nothing left of Dangereuse and just the obedient, matronly shell of Amauberge?

I took a deep breath, cold air striking my lungs. I would go on.

Passing the lodge palisade with its row of pointed stakes, I hastened toward the little dell I remembered from long ago. Aimery had wooed me there as a young bride and we had tumbled amidst the wildflowers, unbridled in our passions, on several moonlit nights. It seemed so long ago. We had become different people, our ways diverging utterly—I grew filled with longing for something *more*, while Aimery became even more like an old man, fidgety and short-tempered, even though he was still nowhere near a greybeard's years.

I proceeded into the dell where I dismounted and tied the mare's reigns to a sturdy oak branch. I stood in my dark cloak staring around. Beneath my feet, the white flowers known as *Ail l'ours* glowed, pale as the moon, emitting a faint but pungent garlicky scent. Legends say bears loved to eat them, digging up their bulbs with their great claws. The Sanglier, the wild boars, also savoured their pungent flavour.

The mist was dissipating even more quickly now, rising up to form a thick ring, like a retaining wall, on the lips of the dell while leaving the shallow bowl below clear of vapours.

I sank down amidst the flowers with their heavy scent. Would he come? Or had this been a fool's errand, an embarrassment for a frivolous woman who should have been at home sewing and tending babes? Nervous, I bit my lip, wondering what the time might be. I had forgotten to listen for the sound of the bells coming from the nearby abbey, and the mist might well have obliterated their tolling anyways. I hoped I was not too late; that William, believing I had lost my nerve, had come and gone…

A noise…In the gloom, I heard a branch crack, the hiss of a boot passing over damp grass. I stared up, saw nothing above, only the trees and the grey-white ring of the thinning mist. I turned in a circle, feeling oddly vulnerable, wanting to call out yet not daring to do so. What if the watcher in the woods was not William? What if it was a brigand who had seen my approach and followed to claim a new victim? I slid my hand down to my side. As part of my male ensemble, I had not only donned mannish garb but fastened a sharp little dagger to my belt. I did not really know how to use such a weapon, but I certainly had no qualms about thrusting it into an enemy's gut if one dared to attack…

Another leafy rustle; a bough swayed, dipping ominously. A red fox ran out of the undergrowth, skittering down the slope, running across to bushes on the other side of the dell. A small laugh broke from my lips as my heartbeat slowed from thunderous to normal. Just a harmless beast of the forest...

An arrow thudded into the earth next to my foot, white-fletched, vibrating with the strength of the impact. Leaping away in fright, I slipped on the wet grass and fell heavily to my knees. I flailed about in the gloom, trying to regain my purchase, fearing I would be shot and killed by archers of my own husband's guard.

And then I heard the sound of laughter. Male laughter, deep and rich. Terror turning to rage, I staggered to my feet. Flinging back my hood, I strode boldly forward. "How dare you, whoever you are! I am Viscountess Dangereuse l'Isle Bouchard. I'll have you whipped..."

"And I might enjoy it!" Grinning like a loon, Duke William of Aquitaine strolled down the side of the dale, bow in hand. "Why are you so angry, Dangereuse? You said in your letter that I could hunt down the fair white doe!"

"I did not mean with an actual weapon!" I kicked at the nearby arrow like a petulant child, breaking the shaft. "You could have killed me."

"Do you doubt my archery skills?"

"I do not know what to think!"

Still smirking, he strode towards me, his eyes sharp as lances, mesmerizing, beads of dew jewelling his curled hair. He was clean-shaven in the Roman fashion; it showed up his strong jaw and Patrician features. I felt my heart begin to dance, my anger waning.

He caught my hand. "Did the sudden fear of imminent death not make you realise how glorious it is to live? "

"I could have done without it," I scoffed, pulling back my hand and folding my arms, almost defensively.

He was beside me, looming over me by several inches, smelling of musk and horse …and, slightly, of wine and firewood. He reached out again to catch my arm, his fingers pressing against the pulse in my wrist. "Death…and love…so closely intertwined." He stroked my flesh with his thumb as if feeling for the very pulse of life.

My brows lifted and my lips parted but I found, for once, my tongue was stilled, not quite understanding his meaning…but thrilling at his touch with its implied sensuality.

"They sometimes call the fulfilment of the act of love a little death, you know…*La petite mort.* In that great pleasure, yet the life force is spent as we head down, as all mortals must, towards death and decay…"

"I am not sure if that is troubadour's talk or…or just grotesque," I murmured.

He chuckled low in his throat. "It makes it all the sweeter, my beautiful Dangereuse, knowing that nothing is forever. We must savour all we can while young, for soon youth will be gone and the tomb and grave worms beckoning."

He put his arms around me, and I sank into his embrace with a sigh. "Were you able to get away from the lodge without being seen?"

He nodded. "I leapt from the window; it wasn't far. Your husband was sound asleep and snoring, dead to the world."

"May he stay so."

William reached out to touch my hair, pulling it free from where it had rucked up inside my hood. "Such beautiful hair…like fire even in the dark. A temptress's hair...but I am surprised. I admit, at first, that your appearance tonight startled me. A man's cloak, a man's breeches, and I see..." he moved a fold of my mantle aide, "a man's tunic and shirt."

"I could hardly have ridden here alone in a gown with my hair flowing out behind me like a comet's tail," I scolded. "It is not a safe journey for a solitary traveller, even for an armed man."

He reached out, unclasping my cloak, and throwing it on the ground as a makeshift blanket. "Still...it is very odd to see such a comely woman dressed in the fashion of a page boy! I am not one of those men who also sports with lads, although I have known a few who do..."

"I do not look like a boy!" I said hotly, insulted.

He shrugged. "I say only as I saw!"

I stepped back from him, tossing back my wild, snarled hair. "I dare you to say I look like some pretty catamite now!"

Reaching to my waist, I grabbed hold of Aimery's tunic and shirt and yanked them over my head.

William stared, eyes feasting hungrily on my nakedness. I stood there boldly, unashamed as Eve in the Garden—but without her innocence.

"No, my lady," the Duke murmured, as he reached for me. "You definitely do not resemble any boy that I have ever seen."

CHAPTER SIX

In the morning, the mist had completely lifted. Red light filtered between the trees, heralding a fine, fair day. Birds sang to herald the coming light and the wildflowers strewn amidst the white carpet of the buckram opened their petals to embrace the dawn.

William and I lay tangled together, the dew warm on our naked skin. I glanced at him, almost shyly; the battle-scarred torso, the muscled legs. The body that had made me an adulteress.

Grunting, William staggered to his feet, roughly hauling on his damp garments. "It is later than I thought. I must get back…we do not want your husband to send a search party."

"What will you tell him if he sees you return?" I struggled up, pulling on my crumpled male garb. My hair was a bird's nest tangle, my body aching and yet sated. I had been given what I desired and did not regret it, but what was to happen now? I was no foolish innocent; I was well aware of William's reputation with women, and also how many men lost interest once they had bedded a woman. The chase, for many, was better than the final capture.

I did not want that to happen. I wanted to leave Aimery, and go to Poitiers with William, even if only as his mistress. Shame? Sin? I cared nothing for that. I would make my confessions, certainly, when the time came, but I would not deny the longings of the body…or the heart.

"Tell him?" William was hopping on one foot, yanking on his boot. "Oh, that I was over-hot and could not sleep. That I staggered out into the woods to piss because someone was shitting in the privy, and fell down in a drunken stupor when I got lost in the mist. Do you think he will believe me?"

"You are his lord—I do not think it matters whether he believes you or not. It is not his place to question—and he knows it, even if he resents it."

"True," William grinned, going for the other boot. "I do not think excess courage—or great passion—are qualities much in evidence in Aimery de Châtellerault."

"And…and what is to become of me?" I said softly. There was no way to broach the subject other than straightforwardness. "What am I to you? A one-night encounter? Or…" I shrugged, the white sleeves of Aimery's oversized shirt flapping like wings.

He stared at me, his eyes burning. "You…you are everything."

"Am I?" I breathed. "Are these but words? How can we resolve this…situation in which we find ourselves?"

"I will have you," he said, his voice suddenly harsh, and he pulled me roughly into his embrace and devoured my mouth with such passion I was sure he might throw me down on the buckram bed and have his way with me again. "But…I cannot walk into the hunting lodge and tell Aimery I have dishonoured his marriage bed. Not because I fear his wrath…but because I do not want your good name to be besmirched…"

"It will be, no matter what," I said. "I will be forever branded a whore."

"It would not reflect so badly on you," said William, with a crafty smile, "if you were carried off from your husband's castle by force. If our liaison was considered no fault of yours."

"William? What have you planned?"

"Let me know when Aimery is away from Châtellerault, embroiled in matters that take him far from home. Once he is out of the way, I will bring a small armed force to your castle. The gates will be opened for me without question because I am lord of Aquitaine You will play the part of doting wife to Aimery and perfect hostess to his guest, and I, foul beast that I am, shall abduct you from your very bed and carry you off to Poitiers."

"Clever!" I said. "I fear they still will consider me a wanton...but no matter. Better a less willing wanton, than an outright bold one, I suppose. And my children will suffer less if it is thought I was taken against my will."

We kissed again, fast, furious, then William pulled away. He glanced up at the sky. "We dare not linger. The sun had long risen. I will go and pacify Aimery, while you head home to Châtellerault. Take care on the road, my beauty." He reached up to touch my cheek, damp with dew. "Ride hard and ride fast for home. May God protect you on your journey."

I rather doubted God would think overmuch of me after I had brazenly committed the sin of adultery, but it was too late to worry about such matters. Perhaps the Virgin would be more amenable to prayers for safe-guarding...though being the eternal virgin, tainted by no sin, possibly not.

I kissed William one more time, his rough unshaven chin abrasive against my lips, and then I lunged for my horse's reins. "I will inform you when Aimery is occupied. Fare you well, until the day when you come to claim what is yours...forever."

Nimbly I swung myself onto the grey mare's back. William watched me admiringly; I had a good seat and rode well, having enjoyed riding astride since youth, unlike some frightened women who slumped in their saddles like sacks full of cabbages, fearful that an invigorating ride would somehow damage their female parts.

"Godspeed," the Duke said, and his hand reach out to strike the mare's hindquarters, making her bound forward, startled. "Now make haste! I can hear the cries of both men and beasts."

I heard them too now—men from the lodge and barking hounds. I must fly or be discovered. Setting my heels to the grey mares flanks, I cantered away into the trees, forcing my way through the overgrown deer trails, making a wide circle around the hunting lodge until I reached the road to Châtellerault.

Like a mad thing, I galloped back towards the castle, my cloak flying behind me in the wind of my speed. There were a few carts on the road at that early hour; the odd pilgrim with hood and staff and badge, an old crone with firewood strapped to her back. They cast a few long stares in my direction but that was all—no one tried to stop me or even called out a greeting. My hood was up, of course, to hide my visage.

Soon the castle of Châtellerault appeared, dull and sombre in the early morn. Although early, it was later than I had hoped; the watch had opened the gates and there was a steady stream of peasants going in and out of the inner bailey. I frowned, toying with my hood to keep it in place. The horse would have to go. I could not just ride in as if I had not a care in the world.

I guided my mount into the narrow alleyway by the tavern. At that hour, the regulars had not arrived to get sotted on the strong ale; through the grimy horn window, I spied the innkeeper's wife, Berthe, sweeping the grimy flagstones with a besom. Dismounting, I quietly led the placid mare up to the tavern's stable and left her there drinking from a trough. I could not come back for her, but she had served her purpose. The innkeeper and his wife would probably claim the Faes had left her as a gift, and as one did not go against the fairy people's will without great personal risk, no need existed to go searching for any possible human owner.

Leaving the tavern precincts before any of the stableboys heard me and came scrambling down from the stable loft, I scurried across the market square, past a thin stream of sleepy merchants, bakers, fishmongers and rat-catchers preparing for their day's work. Mercifully, my disguise held up—mostly because none of them expected to see a noblewoman in men's garb run across their path, let alone their own Viscountess.

Breathing heavily, I slipped around the side of the castle, praying that the postern was still open after my initial passage the night before. Otherwise, I would have to face the gate sentries, like it or not—and tongues would soon wag. Luckily, the postern was merely shut and not locked, exactly as I had left it. Still moving stealthily, I opened it and bolted across the gardens, falling in through the nearest door into the apartments and up the spiralled stairs to the uppermost floor.

Once inside my bedchamber, I slammed the door behind me and slid the bolt. Glancing towards the bed, I saw that my makeshift 'body' was untouched; my subterfuge had not been discovered by my maids. Amused, I pulled off my male garb and threw it into the bottom of a chest, hiding it beneath a raft of folded linens and draperies. Then I dragged on a light chemise and collapsed onto my bed.

I ached all over and felt exhausted—but deliciously so. It was a heady sensation indeed.

Outside I heard the scuffle of shoes in the corridor. "My Lady? Lady Dangereuse?" Pontia's voice came through the crack at the edge of the door. "Are you well? You've been very quiet."

"Go away, girl!" I called out, turning over on my belly. "Let me sleep."

The footsteps retreated hurriedly. No doubt Pontia thought I was still suffering from my unpleasant female malady.

In truth, I had never felt better....

The next few months were agony. I heard nothing from William, but had not truly expected to, as yet—it was too risky. However, the fear was always there that he would view me as just one of his many conquests, lose interest, and pass on to another. Aimery was unsuspecting of what had occurred in the dell beyond the hunting lodge but seemed to have taken on a mysterious additional dislike for his liege lord, grizzling about his behaviour, his unfair demands, at every turn.

I threw myself at my husband, soothing him, telling him—yes, William is a harsh master; so cruel to take so much from Châtellerault in order to pay his troubadour hordes and the painted strumpets in his court. I fawned and caressed, and managed to coax him into regular bedding—something that had eased off since my twin daughters, Aenor and Aois, were born. The thought of another possible pregnancy made me slightly queasy, with what I had planned for the future, but I was concerned that my night with William might bear fruit. Such a thing, if it came to pass, had to be covered up and covered well. As it happened, there were no consequences of my great sin with Duke William, and Aimery was doubtless fully convinced that he had a loyal, loving wife who had eyes only for him…and no interest whatsoever in his overlord.

In September, Aimery announced that before month's end he would head out into his lands to collect the rents. Joy filled me at his words, though I kept my face solemn, and nodded meekly. "How long will you be away, husband?"

He furrowed his brow. "A few weeks. After the rents are collected, I am to check on some drainage ditches that are being dug. Then I must make a stop at the convent— that old hag the Prioress of Lencloitre has been sniping at me because she believes some peasants are regularly poaching in the woods near the abbey. She wants them strung up—she's always full of good Christian cheer—but I am not minded to go on some mad search that will doubtless prove futile. The deer are dead and eaten and the perpetrators long gone. So I'll let her gnaw my ear off with complaints for a few days, nod sympathetically when appropriate, and leave her with that which all sisters of the church desire…"

"Will you? My goodness!" I teased.

He flushed. He had grown so prudish with age and did not enjoy any joke I made that smacked of ribaldry. "I meant *money*, Dangereuse. *Money*. That's what the church loves most—more than Christ, sometimes, or so it seems. God forgive me for my blasphemy."

"Give the abbess my regards," I said sweetly, "and remember to remind her that we are still considering giving Aois to the order when she is old enough. The thought might keep her pleasant."

Aimery nodded, scratching his chin. "Yes, I had almost forgotten about Ais possibly becoming a nun. You are wise, Dangereuse. I know I am not the most attentive man and do not hold with squalling singers or reading foolish romances, which I know you enjoy, but I say this truly—I do not know what I'd do without you as my wife."

"Ooh," I breathed, flushing. I cast my guilty gaze to the floor. For a moment, I felt a pang of sympathy for my dullard husband, but suddenly he spoilt the moment, and my sympathy vanished like morning mist.

"While I am gone, see to it that the castle is cleaned top to toe, will you? The privies are setting up an awful stink."

"If you wish, husband…but usually we remove to another castle with the children for the cleaning."

"Yes, but I'd like it done before my return. I do not fancy the hurly-burly of a move to one of our manors before year's end. You can handle it—you are very efficient, for a woman. As I said, I don't know what I'd do without you. You are good at getting necessary things done."

He patted me on the arm, like a child, and stalked away, mind clearly on his meeting with the hated Prioress.

I clenched my hands. If my worth was no more than getting the garderobes cleaned when the mess and upheaval would not bother him, then I would be glad to depart and let him find some equally efficient skivvy from amongst the town's wenches.

Fool is the man who takes his woman for granted…

CHAPTER SEVEN

Aimery rode away into the foggy September morn, unsuspecting. Furiously I waved goodbye from the battlements—maybe for the last time. Perhaps guilt should have risen up to stop what I sought to do, but it didn't. Beside me, the children stood in a line, also waving, except for those too small to peek between the crenels. I gestured for the nurse to lift up Aois and Aenor, who were the smallest. Looking at them, I did feel a pang of regret, but the children would survive, Poitiers was not so far away. I had no idea how Aimery would react to my 'abduction,' but I doubted he would do more than curse and bluster for fear of offending his sworn lord. To go against William would be pure folly; a fight he could not win and one likely to see his head upon a spike.

I hurried from the walls as Aimery's company faded into the distance. The nursemaids went the other way, shepherding the children, who were all hungry and calling for treats, in the direction of the nursery tower. I was hungry too—hungry to get my new, dangerous adventure started.

As before, I appropriated Aimery's seal and sent a message to William, ostensibly from Aimery, telling him that he would be away and therefore unable to receive his lordship should he wish to meet. I sketched out the possible time Aimery might be away and where, then sent the message off by my favourite courier, who was happily both discreet and dully loyal and unlikely to suspect anything was amiss.

Once the messenger had ridden for Poitiers, I set about my daily duties to keep suspicion away and to calm my own nerves. For three days I continued thus, overseeing those damn privies being sluiced and making lists of bacon and flour and spices. In the evening, weary, I would stand on the walls watching the sunset, pretending to take the air before bed, but in truth watching the horizons for any signs of William's approach. I saw only nightbirds flapping up into the smoky, sun-bloodied haze.

On the day after the Feast of Michaelmas, sacred to the angels Michael, Gabriel and Raphael, my lover finally came to claim me. I had eaten the customary Michaelmas dish of roast goose and mutton pie followed by waffles and blackberry tarts, and then, with nought more to do, retired to my bed. I lay beneath the coverlet, clad only in my thin chemise, while Pontia and Eustachie lay on paillasses near the fire brazier, whispering together for a while before falling silent and beginning to snore. I was restless, tossing and turning. Would he come tonight? Or would he not, perhaps not ever? Would I moon about like a lovestruck maiden, only to have Aimery return and my dull, unfulfilled life with him resume till the end of my days?

"Where, by Christ's Beard, are you?" I muttered to myself.

And then I heard a clamour of men's voices in the bailey. Loud, urgent, but not raised in anger. Surprised voices, confused shouts. I wanted to leap up and peer from the window but was afraid that if I were spotted, it might arouse suspicions. Breathing heavily, sweat starting to gather on my brow, I lay still beneath the embroidered quilt, straining to hear what was going on outside.

The hubbub grew louder. Now the voices were less friendly, more concerned. Horses began to neigh and armour jingled. I heard a man cry out, his tone commanding, "Hold, you, hold back; put aside your swords! Duke William is your master's liege lord and what you do is treasonous! Away from the Duke, and you all shall go unharmed. Fight his will, and this castle will go up in flames with every man, woman and child inside."

The maids awoke, bleary-eyed, on their paillasses as these last shouts rang out. Frightened, they clung to each other. "God help us!" wailed Eustachie. "We might be taken and ravished and butchered."

"Hush!" I said from the bed, trying to calm them both. "Did you not hear the words that were spoken? It is Count William. He is a good lord—he will not hurt us."

"But…but this is abnormal!" wept Pontia. "Why has he come in such a manner? It's night and he has burst in unannounced like a brigand about to pillage and burn, and his captain is threatening as much."

"Well, clearly he *is* angry," I said. "Aimery must have done something to upset him. I am sure he will take what he needs as recompense and then go about his way…"

Both maids looked dubious and remained terrified. I thought their eyes might start from their sockets as loud, scuffling footsteps sounded in the corridor outside the bedchamber. Men's footsteps, heavy and determined.

"You…you cannot pass…" I heard one of the servants cry weakly.

I cursed. Pray the little fool stood out of the way before he got himself killed!

I heard a slap and a thud and then pained whining. The newcomers had knocked him down. At least the man was still alive!

The next moment, a mailed fist struck the door, making it shudder. Pontia and Eustachie screeched and clung even more tightly to each other.

"Open...open it, I command you!" It was William's voice that roared out, filling me with shivering excitement. I dared not show it, though. I had to play my part of the offended lady of the manor.

"Count William...is that you?" I cried, sitting up and holding the coverlet against my chest in a suitably modest fashion. "How dare you come here when my lord is away and burst into my castle like this! It is most dishonourable."

"Be silent!" His bellow was like a bear's roar yet, underneath, I could detect a hint of merriment. He was enjoying the charade.

"Dishonour? That, Madam, is what your husband has done to me. He is a dishonourable churl!"

I was tempted for a moment to ask what Aimery had 'done' that was so dreadful but was afraid the situation might become ridiculous—so much so that any witnesses would realise how much of it was staged.

"Let me *iiin!*" William roared again, resuming his frenzied pounding. The bar across the door jumped and juddered. The two maids were sobbing and praying.

"Portia...listen to me; get a hold of yourself. The Duke has no quarrel with you, only with the Viscount. Get up...open the door."

"But my Lady," she wept, "what if he kills us all?"

"He has no reason to kill us," I said, but she looked so stricken and faint, I shouted out to William, "Promise, good Duke, that no harm will come to my attendants."

"I promise, I promise! Now come along, open up, before I change my mind!"

Eustachie clambered up and ran to my side. "Madame, I am confused and afraid...He swears he will not harm us, but why does he want to be in your bedchamber, if his quarrel is only with Lord Aimery?"

Damn…she was thinking too much for one in abject fear.

I patted her shoulder. "I fear I must deal with him in his lordship's absence."

"I beg you…no! You are in…an unseemly state. He sounds…wild, uncontrolled!"

"If I refuse, he will only smash the door down and be even more wrathful." I turned my head. "Pontia, you heard what I told you—open the door!"

Sobbing hysterically, Pontia stumbled to her feet and threw off the latch. Immediately the door crashed inwards, slamming against the wall so hard that one of the hinges gave way and hung down at a crooked angle.

In stormed William of Aquitaine, clad in a heavy mail shirt, his severe helmet with its sharp nose guard hiding most of his visage and giving him a stern, almost inhuman appearance. Just two dark, glittering eyes framed by shining metal. Behind him were half a dozen armed men, equally ferocious, their weapons drawn.

Pontia ran across the chamber, grabbing Eustachie's arm and pulling her into a corner, where they crouched, squealing and weeping.

William and his soldiers paid the maids no heed. My lover strode to the bed and yanked the coverlet out of my hands with a grand flourish. "Onto your feet, Lady Dangereuse!" he ordered.

I pretended to quaver in fear before him, well aware that my maids' terrified eyes were fastened upon me. "My Lord, swear you will treat me well, for I have done nothing and was no part of my husband's wrongdoing, whatever that might be."

"I will treat you as I wish," he thundered, "for Aimery de Châtellerault holds that which is truly mine! I will carry you hence as my payment for the ills he has committed against his lord!"

The two girls began to wail even louder, imploring him in the name of the Virgin to release me unharmed. William's eyes, beneath that jutting nosepiece, were glittering with unbridled glee. "From this day forth, Lady Dangereuse, you will be my concubine—to serve me in my chamber...and in my bed!"

More desolate shrieks and howls emanated from the corner.

William grabbed my arm; his movement was sharp, yet those mailed fingers light as a feather. "Come, do not resist or it will go the worse for you!"

"But my Lord Duke..." I pretended to sway as if about to collapse in a faint. "This is evil, sinful...diabolical! To carry me off from my bed, a happily wedded matron...and I almost naked in my shift."

"Be silent!" he said. "Or I shall rip off even that flimsy covering and make you walk out before all men's eyes into the castle yard."

"You would not dare!" I breathed. I was not, at that point, certain if he was jesting or not.

"I do as I please." He yanked me to him, his mouth claiming mine in a hard kiss, then he lifted me up in his arms and threw me over his shoulder like a sack.

Pontia and Eustachie started screaming anew, as tears sprang from their eyes and drenched their cheeks.

Lying over William's mailed shoulder, he kept trying to surreptitiously tickle me, and I tried to control my laughter by pretending to sob. Borne aloft in this undignified fashion, my lover carried me from the castle apartments into the bailey. The household servants crowded around, shouting curses and imprecations at William, but

Aimery's guards stood aside, shame-faced, weapons laid down, knowing they dared not spar with the Duke's men.

I was carried, William's prize, through the open gates and into the town centre where a huge mob of townsfolk had gathered, hissing and spitting, but not daring to begin a full-fledged riot. There was a chariot waiting, surrounded by ducal soldiers. William lifted me from his shoulder and dumped me inside on a pile of cushions, telling me to keep down and keep quiet. Then he let the heavy curtains fall and I was left alone.

A few minutes later, the wheels below began to move and the carriage juddered forward over the uneven cobbles. There was shouting, booing and a small, brief, and rather insipid clash of weaponry, followed by a scream of pain and another loud round of renewed booing.

Then the sounds of the town and its angry residents faded into the distance, and I heard only the clop of hooves, the tinkle of horse harness, the snorting of the beasts that pulled the chariot. I lay shivering in my thin chemise, genuinely cold but also feeling a sense of anticipation.

I was going to my new home. I was going to live, wanton woman that I was, with my lover, the Count of Poitou and Duke of Aquitaine.

CHAPTER EIGHT

"Stand there." I moved uncertainly, blind. Willian's hands were clamped over my eyes. "Now—look up."

The hands fell away. We stood together in the courtyard of Poitiers palace, gazing up at a great new tower with a conical red turret and white-washed facing stones that blazed in the sunlight.

I glanced at my lover, eyebrows raised in silent question. Upon our arrival at Poitiers, he had insisted I get down from the chariot despite my scanty garb and walk through the bailey with my eyes hidden. Mercifully, he had realised I needed his cloak—for decency if not for warmth! But the palms had remained over my eyes till now. I was not sure what he was showing me. It was a handsome building but it was not as though I had no knowledge of fine castles.

"This is yours," he said. "I had started to build soon after I first saw you...and wanted you. I called it *La Maubergeon,* after you."

"You know Amauberge is a name of my past."

"I know, my sweeting, but I could hardly call it the 'Dangerous Tower', could I? Men would think it a place for torture or imprisonment when it is truly a place for love to blossom." He reached for my hand, giving it a hard squeeze. "Come, let me show you the rest of the palace, Dangereuse."

We walked together into the Great Hall. It was the longest Hall I had ever seen, its roof constructed of huge oak timbers. "We call it the Hall of Lost Footsteps," grinned William, "for one cannot hear the approach of anyone from the far end so long and so high it is."

We passed from the hall into the ducal apartments—and what I saw was wondrous to my eyes. Some years before, William had ridden on Crusade in the Holy Land, and it seemed this journey had greatly influenced his tastes. Silks hung draped on the walls and across the round-headed windows, luxurious in azure, sapphire, dawn-blue, crimson, damson and sun-gold. Imported carpets from Spain and Turkey, zigzagged with exotic patterns, lay across the floors, while the ceilings were midnight-blue and painted with stars.

From there, we strolled arm in arm to the gardens at the rear of the palace. Columns like those of a Greek or Roman temple bounded the edges of a long pool filled with aquamarine water. Little conduits fed it from some hidden spring, bubbling and splashing. All around were vine-heavy trellises and riotous flowers, climbing and twining, forming a floral canopy.

"It is magical." I knelt and let my hand drift below the surface of the pool. The water was so clear, so pure, icy against my palm. At the bottom, tiles were arranged in the shapes of fish, birds and cavorting nymphs.

Someone began to strum on a lyre, and a troupe of musicians emerged from behind a manicured hedge. A troubadour in peacock array wandered behind them, singing in Occitan.

"How wonderful!" I breathed. I thought of my life back at Châtellerault and it seemed so dark and mean and ordinary. Here…I had walked into a realm of light and beauty. Music and poetry had always touched my soul and here it was around me, living and wonderful, no longer an idle fantasy.

Smiling, William took my elbow. "You can come back later, Dangereuse. First, I want to see you established and comfortable in your tower. And you cannot go walking about much longer in a soiled chemise…"

"No…quite true. It might cause talk, though I dare say less than if I hurled it off and bathed in that lovely pool…as I would love to do."

"You will have your own bath, Dangereuse. I will show you. No need to cavort in a garden water-feature."

He led me back to the Maubergeon Tower, and we entered on the ground floor, using a key to access the rooms beyond. In most castles, the lowest floor would merely be a storage area, but here there was a sunken stone bath in the midst of polished green tiles streaked with white marble. Water was pumped into it, perhaps using some old Roman conduit, and it was scented with roses. Amethyst-hued walls glimmered in the light of half a dozen candelabra.

"Here is a bath fit for Cleopatra," said William proudly. "You can bathe here in asses' milk, even as she did…and I will join you, even as her lovers, the great Caesar and the mighty Marc Anthony, did in ancient times."

Leaving the bath chamber, we ascended a winding staircase. At the top were my personal apartments, draped in green silks and linens so that they resembled a forest—an echo of our first night as lovers. The ceiling was domed and, like William's own rooms in the main palace, painted to resemble the night sky with hundreds of golden stars and a crescent moon. There was a painted screen with the image of a dragon-slayer, perhaps St George, rescuing a naked, golden-haired maiden who was bound to a rock, and a wide bed of dark wood carved with strange and sensuous beings, satyrs and mermaids and the god Bacchus, priapic and lewd, with a cluster of grapes in his hand and a nude maiden at his knee. Wine-dark curtains threaded with bronze hung around the bed, giving privacy to whoever lay inside.

A large chest stood by the screen. William beckoned me over and cast back the lid. Inside were gowns of various hues, their hems and bodices shimmering with gemstones or embroidered with gold, the sleeves lined with marten or red and grey squirrel. Beneath these lay piles of undergarments made of fine linen.

"I am sure you can find something in here to your taste," William said. "I had to guess the size of your…*proportions* from our little encounter. If I am wrong, I will have the tailor adjust them. I have also chosen two ladies to attend to your needs and they are also skilled with the needle."

I pulled out a gown the hue of cherries, its long sleeves made of tawny silk. "I think I shall wear this today. What do you think?"

He caught me round the waist, his laughter rich and throaty. "First I want you out of *that*…"

There was a hiss as the ribbons lacing my chemise gave way and the garment fell to the floor.

"And I think we should test the comfort of that new bed I bought especially for you."

Adjusting to life in the splendour of Poitiers palace was surprisingly easy. Occasionally I thought of the children back in Châtellerault, but I was sure their nurses and tutors would keep them occupied. I also thought of Aimery once or twice, and that left a sour taste in my mouth. I knew he would have to say something about my 'abduction', lest men laugh at him as a cuckold, but I had no idea how he would go about it. I prayed he would not do something foolish, feeling his honour as a man was besmirched, such as trying to storm Poitiers with an army. He did not have enough men to take such a strongly defended town; it would be like a puppy snapping at the paws of a mighty lion. Even worse, if he attacked his liege lord he would be committing treason, and his life would be forfeit. I did not want my children to lose their father...

It was with trepidation that one day, outside by the pool, listening to a poet speak pretty words of unrequited love, I heard the gate sentries cry out and caught sight of one of Aimery's banners. Leaving the poet to mope, I wrapped my mantle around my shoulders and hurried into the donjon. I slid along a little corridor that William had shown me, which snaked behind the high seat in the audience chamber. Shielded from view by a heavy red curtain, I peeped through a gap. I recognised the messenger in Aimery's colours, a trusted man name Arold. He knelt before William, handing him a rolled-up parchment.

William slowly unrolled it, his lips pursing as his gaze skimmed the contents. Arold was sweating, clearly ill at ease, fearful of his reaction. After a moment or two, William cleared his throat. "Well, well, well...Aimery Viscount of Châtellerault is most put out that his wife has left him. No threats of warfare—he is smarter than that—but 'This is an abhorrent act, the act of a tyrant'? Strong words! And this—'I demand her return and compensation'. Well, messenger, you may go back and tell him that Dangereuse de L'isle Bouchard is not goods to be traded. And as for this ludicrous last statement—'I will appeal to higher powers if you do not return my wife to her rightful lord.' What, is he going to ask God to smite me down? I am sure he would not be the first to ask. No, return home to Châtellerault, and tell your master that I expect his full obedience, and that Lady Dangereuse will not return. Tell him, though, that because I am a kindly and honest lord, some compensation for his loss will be sent to him in due time."

"M-my Lord Duke?" stammered Arold, face white and queasy beneath a sheen of sweat. "How can I…I…"

"You heard me. You've taken it all in, I assume. Those are my terms and the Viscount will have to accept them. He has no choice. Go now, and bother me no more."

Arold bowed and scurried from the audience chamber while I emerged from my hiding place, laughing.

William turned in his seat to look at me. "Ah, you were eavesdropping. I thought you might be."

"I believe in knowledge, not ignorance. It can forestall many unpleasant issues. Speaking of which, what do you suppose Aimery meant by 'higher powers'?"

William shrugged. "You doubtless know better than I. Is he a very pious man?"

"Not particularly. Not enough to believe a lightning bolt will drop from the sky to smite you if he asks the Almighty nicely enough."

"All bluster then; I am certain of it. Put thoughts of his threats from your radiant head, Dangereuse—I am going to put them from mine."

I did as my lover bid, which was not hard at all. Aimery, even in high dudgeon, was just not memorable. I wondered how I had ever thought him attractive as a girl. My attention now was all on William, and for the marvellous books he had in his library, and for his fellow troubadours, learned and yet not dull and stolid, telling the tales and singing the songs of great heroes and epic tragedies, alongside earthy, bawdy songs about courtesans and harlots. They flocked to me like bees to honey, putting me on a high pedestal, a queen of love that they dared not touch, and oh, yes, it was sweet indeed.

But, of course, just as in all the old romantic tales, heaven had its shadow…

In this case, it was the shadow of a woman.

And the woman was William's wedded wife.

I'd almost forgotten about the Duchess Philippa. Whenever William spoke of her, I envisioned a dusty stick of a woman, jaundiced and uninteresting, swaddled in dark robes like some ancient walking lich. That was how he had made her sound when he mentioned her—which was not often. Dull Philippa, plain Philippa, prudish Philippa who had no fire in her belly or anywhere else that mattered. Philippa, who was far from Poitiers, sulking or praying or both.

So, I reacted with startlement and alarm when a large entourage arrived at Poitiers Palace, horning blaring, and was admitted without question or even the smallest delay.

I was watching in the window of the Maubergeon, and behind me, William was cursing and struggling into his clothing. "Who is this?" I asked, frowning, as I peered down at the well-armed men in the courtyard, gathered around what appeared to be a very fine chariot. "They've come right in without a challenge and they are dismounting. You weren't expecting them…obviously."

I glanced over my shoulder as he hopped around one-legged, yanking on the second half of his trousers, and then bawled another oath as he struck his toe on the brazier.

"I was not expecting anyone," he said when he was done. "Dangereuse, do not be angry...but it appears that my wife Philippa has decided to pay me a visit."

"Oh, has she now? You told me she was mainly based in Toulouse these days, along with your children."

"Well, that is not a lie, Dangereuse, if that's what you are implying," he said testily. "I did not think she would much care to return to Poitiers. Last time I saw her, she said she'd had enough of my whoring. Fear not, you do not have to meet her. I shall deal with her demands and send her packing as swiftly as I can."

My nostrils flared. "I am not a coward, William. If I am more than a mere bed-mate for you, then I will look your estranged wife in the face as an equal. Do you not agree?"

He looked slightly flummoxed. "Oh yes, yes, whatever you wish—just do not end up in some uncouth catfight in the Hall."

"Aha," I said. "You fear we might come to blows? So Philippa is not the timid creature you portrayed her as."

"Did I portray her as such? Or was that what you hoped?" He glanced at me slant-wise. "You *wanted* to hear that she was dull as ditch-water with a horse's face and udders like a cow. A woman who paled to nothing beside the beauteous Dangereuse!" He smirked and grabbed me, swinging me around; I was in a sleeping robe which whirled open, giving him a glimpse of my white limbs beneath. "And in that, you would be right—she does pale beside you, as do all others. But she is not uncomely to behold and she is not stupid, either. Now I will go to her, and find out her need. Wait till the Terce bell rings and then come to the hall to present yourself."

He left the chamber and I called for my ladies to dress me. I wanted to look my finest, so chose green silk which went well with my flaming hair. Sadly, my locks could not flow free without remark, so instead the maids braided it multiple times and then placed a sheer flimsy veil over it, with a silver circle to hold its abundance in place. I put on my best slippers, a similar green to my dress, etched with gold, and a fancy girdle studded with big blue cabochons.

Trying to assume a serene and queenly air, I put my chin high in the air and glided towards the hall—a rustle of verdant silk, a trail of orange and jasmine scent.

As I approached the doorway into the Hall, I noticed the armed sentries on either side were red-faced and holding back loud sniggers. As they spied me, they grew instantly solemn, drawing themselves up to attention.

It soon became evident why they were amused. Another few strides closer and I could hear a woman berating William like some common fishwife.

It could only be the fragrant Philippa.

Gracefully, I stepped into the Hall, my long sleeves swishing.

William sat on the dais, a looked of bemusement on his face. Philippa stood in front of him, gesticulating wildly as she shouted out her frustrations at his behaviour. "I got to Toulouse, and what do you do? You move a harlot into the castle. Into *MY* home? You have shamed and embarrassed me before all men! How dare you!"

I slid along the wall, amid the frozen servants, some appearing genuinely horrified, others barely holding back their mirth like the sentries. The troubadours were eyeing each other, no doubt imagining what kind of songs they could devise about this confrontation.

I fixed my gaze on my rival. She was not my equal in beauty, but yes, she was not as plain as I had imagined. She was quite tall and stocky but neither plump nor raddled. Her raiment was a dull orange-brown colour, but it was well-tailored and of good quality cloth. Her headdress framed her face and had a dangling fringe of amber-hued beads like drops of honey; it looked strange and exotic and I wondered if William had brought it from the Holy Land as a gift. But her face entranced me more, strong-boned with winged dark brows and flashing amber eyes. Not a beautiful face, but a handsome one with character. I found character more admirable in a woman than the simpering of the vacuous, limp, blonde maids many men claimed to prefer. Weak as watery piss, such women seemed to me.

Philippa had not noticed my presence. She continued to shake her fist at William, going on and on about the sacrifices she had made for him, and how her children were embarrassed by his lascivious behaviour. "Yes, I always knew you bedded anything you could get your hands on…but as long as your lewdness was not displayed beneath my nose, it was no concern of mine. But now, you make me a laughing stock, and your own children too…"

Children… At that moment, I noticed the petulant Little Willy standing at his mother's shoulder, looking even more pimply and sulky than I remembered. And, unfortunately, as I looked at him, he turned his head and stared straight back at me.

Immediately his eyes burned with righteous wrath. Little shite! He pointed at me with a quivering finger and yowled like an angry cat—"Mother, she's here. Father's trollop is here, gawping at you like the brazen hussy she is!"

Philippa whirled about with an audible gasp…and then she was storming towards me. William leapt from his chair but hovered in the background.

"How dare you come in when I am talking to my husband?" she snarled. "This is my house, and you are not welcome in it."

"It is Duke William's home," I said calmly, "and you left it of your own volition. Now it is mine. The Maubergeon tower is even named for me."

"Have you no decency at all?" Philippa continued, a flush riding high on her cheekbones. "This is immoral and sinful. Your lover is married and you are wed to Aimery de Châtellerault. That makes your crimes even worse than if you were unwed or a widow. You have children too. How sad for them that one day they must call their mother whore."

"My children will not be so judgmental and stupid, I would hope," I returned.

"You are shameless!" snapped Philippa.

"I am as God made me." I shrugged. "I am happy with my lot—are you? Perhaps you should seek some joy…somewhere else."

"I will leave this den of sin, as it is clear I am no longer wanted in any way. But do not think you and my dog of a husband will get away so lightly with your adultery. Many will take my part, as I am the one who has been wronged, the one who is pure and blameless." She smiled smugly. "I will make sure you regret the day you ever set your hot, lecherous eyes on each other."

I wondered if Philippa had perhaps devised some plan against me with Aimery's assistance. A pity, if that was the case, she had not decided to replace William with my husband, not only as an ally but also as a lover. Yet, looking at the ostentatious golden cross hanging from her neck, I supposed she might find the thought of a physical alliance with a more suitable man far too 'sinful.'

William tried to appeal to Philippa's better nature (if she had one, which I strongly doubted looking at that determined chin.) "Hark to me, Philippa, this friction is unnecessary. You have not lived with me for many months. You know that as long as you remain my wife you shall have income and honour. I do not seek to punish you, for I know the fault is all mine—it is just the way I am…"

"Yes! Weak!" spat Philippa, eyes flashing gold fire. She grabbed the heavy chain of her crucifix and for a moment I thought she might lunge at William, wielding her religion as a weapon quite literally. But if she had envisioned beating her straying husband with the symbol of Christ's suffering, she thought the better of it in the end and let her hand fall away.

William ignored her outburst and continued, "The children will of course be provided for. Young William shall come to Poitiers and have the best tutors and knightly training…"

"No! I require *nothing* from you, Father!" shouted the ill-tempered adolescent, fists curling in childish fury. "You know that! I would rather deal with a…a leper…or a…a PEASANT!"

William frowned at his outspoken boy and Philippa thrust the lad behind her in a theatrical manner, as if she was protecting her infant boy from a ravening lion. "You don't have to take anything from him, Will. My own family have plenty. They shall see you have all that a young nobleman needs. And eventually, when your father passes…to Hell where all fornicators and libertines surely go, especially unrepentant ones, you will have all he owns anyway by right of inheritance. So, the victory will be ours in the end. As for your sire's harlot, if she is still here when that day comes, which I doubt as William's affections are short-lived, I will have her stripped and beaten from the gates and then I will dismantle that cursed tower of hers stone by stone."

William cleared his throat and folded his arms. "I think I have heard more than enough from you, Madam," he said in a tone ice-cold. "If you have nothing more to say…"

"I will go." She tossed her head and grabbed Little Willy's podgy arm. "But believe me, you adulterous, conniving beasts, this is not the last you have heard from me."

She stalked from the hall, Willy thudding after her like Behemoth, while all the household stared in shock. A few moments later, we heard her raised voice shouting commands to her companions in the bailey and then the sound of drumming hoofs as they departed in all speed.

"Do you think her threat an idle one?" I asked, turning to William.

"Maybe…maybe not." He reached for my hand. "But it does not matter. I have repudiated her in public—and whatever she might try, I will never let you go."

CHAPTER NINE

It seemed the trouble Philippa was wishing upon us was…the Pope. A letter arrived from the Pontiff commanding William to return me to Aimery without delay. No arguments would be permitted. A refusal would lead to excommunication.

"What shall we do?" I frowned as I stood before the fire in the bedchamber while William sprawled across a fur-lined window seat, reading the unfriendly missive that had come from Rome.

He glanced up and then he flicked the parchment into the fireplace. It coiled, curled, then went up in a puff of smoke and burst of flame. "Nothing, Dangereuse."

"Nothing? But if we ignore him, you will be…"

"Cut off from the Church; denied the Body of Christ and hence salvation. God's Teeth, Dangereuse, I am already going to burn in Hell for all the fornication and revelry I enjoy! There's a devil waiting to spear my unholy arse with a trident, of this I have no doubt."

"Oh, William, do not speak so." Although neither of us was conventionally pious and both aware of our sinfulness, I still believed in redemption and that many sins might be forgiven. I did not want to burn in the pits of fire, nor did I want my lover to suffer that fate. He was not a bad man really, and he had crusaded for Christ, after all.

"It's too late anyway," said William, leaning back in his seat."

"Too late? What do you mean?"

"The Pope's memory is short, my beloved. I have *already* been excommunicated!"

"Truly?" My brows shot up in surprise. "When did this happen? And why?"

"It happened the year before I brought you to Poitiers. Over taxes. I violated the tax privileges of the church. They said 'Pay up.' I said 'Go swive yourselves.'"

"You did not say such a thing."

"I most certainly did. Bishop Peter, the sour-faced old crow, was sent hence to pronounce the Anathema. In he came with his doom-bell and candles, looking like some walking revenant. I wanted to put my fist into his face but I restrained myself."

I was quite enjoying this story now, even if, I suspected, it might be slightly embellished. I sank to the floor on a tasselled cushion, leaning against my lover's leg. "Oh, do go on. I am intrigued."

"Instead of kneeling at his smelly feet and kissing them, I drew my sword and told him I'd cut off his head if he did not give me absolution for my sins."

"*What*!" I shrieked, genuinely scandalised. "Drawing a sword on a bishop is worse than threatening him with your fist!"

He shrugged. "In any case, he got the better of me, sword or no. He pretended to give me absolution—then the moment I stepped towards the door, he turned around and yammered out the blasted Anathema as fast as his tongue would allow! I couldn't reach him in time to halt him, and so…I was duly excommunicated."

"He must have been braver than most churchmen to have done what he did when you held a sword in your hand."

"Indeed. Once he'd finished, he walked up to me, bent his head and exposed his neck, saying, "I've done what I came here to do. Strike if you must." And I tell you, I was tempted, but there would only be even greater trouble if I had smitten him. Not worth the aggravation. So I sheathed my blade and told him that I did not love him enough to send him to paradise."

I snorted with laughter, almost falling backwards with mirth. Our two hounds, Diamant and Fleury, sat up, woken from sleep, their ears pricked. Seeing no dainties were being thrown for their pleasure, they gave exasperated dog-sighs and lay back down again, disappointed.

But then I grew more serious. "I did not know any of this. I realised you did not attend Mass as often as I but sometimes you did accompany me, and nothing was said. The priest did not drive you from the door."

"My chaplain is loyal. I attend Mass as I wish. I have paid him well."

"You, my lord, are incorrigible."

"And that is why you love me."

I laughed again. "Perhaps. But I sense that this sort of behaviour will bring trouble. Or, should I say, *more* trouble?"

"What trouble? Philippa? She will cool down soon enough and go her own way. She has our children; she has plenty of wealth and lands around Toulouse."

I shook my head. "You really do not understand. She is a woman. Your rejection burns her like a brand. She will desire revenge."

He shrugged. "Well, let her do her worst. And the Pope too. I am not afraid of either."

I pretended to share his fearlessness, but in truth, I felt a growing sense of concern. I was not like other women; I did not care what people thought of my actions—not anymore. My choice was made.

But to go against a great power like the Pope?

Madness.

I shivered, even though the fire was blazing in the brazier.

The papal legate Giraud arrived at Poitier with much fanfare. He had a huge contingent of soldiers surrounding him to impress his might upon us.

"I think you should retire, Dangereuse," William said, staring down from the height of the donjon at the newcomers milling like a hive of ants in the castle bailey. "It seems our friend Giraud is very determined."

Eyes flashing, I turned on my lover. "I do not care how determined he might be, William. If he is here to discuss my presence in your home and your bed, I want to have my say. I am not some dumb ox to be passed here and there to whichever owner the Pope and his legate deem most worthy."

William sighed. "I thought you would say that. Very well. You may accompany me to greet Giraud as I will get no peace otherwise. Promise me you will keep your temper in check. You know how these self-righteous churchmen are. All finger-waggling and full of condemnation—when half of them have a brood of illegitimate brats hidden away in convents and monasteries."

"I worry about *your* temper more than mine," I said, "after hearing about that incident with the sword and Bishop Peter. If I promise to hold my tongue, will you promise no swords…or knives?"

He rolled his eyes. "I promise. I will *not* promise, though, to refrain from braining him with a candlestick should he give you grave insult."

Within the hour, we met with the papal legate in William's private closet. Giraud was a short, thin man, not old but appearing aged owing to his baldness—not a single strand of hair grew on his head. He resembled, to my mind, an egg with ears. An unappealing egg covered in brown speckles from where the sun had caught him hatless. He frowned when he saw me, seemingly disconcerted by a woman's presence. He had thick dark purple lips like two pieces of liver in a skull-shaped yellow face spotted like his pate.

I was wearing my most modest attire, a plain cream bliaut with an unostentatious girdle and a severe white linen wimple that showed no hair at all. William, however, was dressed in almost regal splendour, gleaming with gems, asserting his importance through a display of his wealth.

"Sit, your Grace," William said, gesturing to a rare wooden chair draped in furs.

The papal legate slumped into it. "I would prefer to stand, you understand," he said peevishly, "but I have been riding all day and my bones ache."

"I can have my ladies draw a nice bath for you," I offered, my tone full of sweet innocence. "I am sure they would not mind washing down the back of one so holy."

Scandalised, he stared at me. "No woman shall ever touch me so with her dirty, sinful hands!" he barked. "In fact, I have taken an oath to bathe but once a year as a penance."

"So that's what that smell is," William mumbled under his breath.

I nudged him with my elbow—discretely. Giraud glanced from William to me, eyes narrowed with righteous dislike. His heavy lips quivered. "You know, Duke William, why I am here. Your behaviour is a disgrace to your title. You have been excommunicated once. The Pope is happy to have Anathema pronounced on you once again if you continue in your dissolute ways. This is the second time, my lord, and it will be made fully public across France and across the Christian world—there will be no chance of any forgiveness to follow."

The legate stepped in my direction. "And you, Lady—you should be ashamed. Abiding in sin with this man…in this house of paynim luxuries and effete singers!"

William's nostrils flared. "She had no choice. I carried her off from her husband's castle."

Great tenderness filled me as I heard his words. He lied to defend my honour. I wanted to kiss him but that would hardly help our cause with Legate Giraud.

"I have heard that tale but there is reason not to believe it. Many have seen you laugh…and cavort together. She certainly does not look like an abused prisoner, a victim of your carnal lust. From what I've heard, she enjoys your attentions…her, a mother of five…"

"You seem to have 'heard' a lot," I said, unable to control myself despite earlier avowals. "Is that what His Holiness's Legates do these days—listen to gossip?"

"By your sharp, shrewish tongue, I am proven right," Giraud retorted triumphantly. "Your eyes should be on the ground, woman, in humility and penitence. Instead, they glare out of your face like Jezebel's own! For shame!"

Angrily, he turned back to William. "Enough of this pointless talk and ridiculous excuses. You will return the Viscountess Amauberge to Aimery of Châtellerault, or you pay the penalty of permanent exclusion from the church. In fact, I demand that you send her forth tonight; I will oversee her removal, to make sure it is done."

A flush rose up William's neck and into his cheeks; I saw his muscles tense. "You presume too much, Legate Giraud. Far too much. Curls will grow on that shiny pate of yours before I let Dangereuse go. Do you understand?"

"You have made your choice!" cried Giraud, his voice growing high and shrill. "A stupid choice born of lust! You will suffer the consequences…"

"*You* may suffer consequences too!" William growled, taking a menacing step towards the Legate. I realised he would not be able to hold his temper in check any more than I had kept mine, despite our avowals, and grasped his arm in a tight hold.

"Peace, William," I whispered with urgency.

He shook me off and took another purposeful step towards the Legate Giraud. The churchman, suddenly nervous and sweating, spun around and hurried for the stairs out of the donjon.

William pulled free of me and pursued him, casting me a glance over his shoulder. He was not going to hurt the damned man, but he cared nothing of giving him a serious fright.

Down the stairs they both ran, shoes clattering on the stonework. I followed after, ready to intervene if William did lose control. I paused in the tower doorway as he pursued the legate out through the main gate. He then made a gesture to the sentries in the watch towers above and the portcullis banged down with a rattle of massive chains.

Immediately the legate charged back, gripping the bars with his bony hands, looking half a madman. Men within the bailey started laughing—a titter at first, rising to a roar. "You lock me out? The mouthpiece of his Holiness? You will pay for this, you Godless heathen! Clearly your crusading taught you nothing; you picked up the filthy ways of the paynim."

"What are you going to do?" I murmured to William as I walked. "He's outside...but his entourage is within." I nodded toward the crowds of men gathered miserably by the outbuildings. The churchmen and servants merely looked horrified, but the rest, and their numbers were great, were soldiers, fierce in appearance, whose stony gazes were locked on William's archers, who had arrows trained upon them from the walls. "We could still be in trouble here."

"Do not fear, I will deal with it," said William. He strode toward the gate, almost ending up nose to nose with the enraged legate through the cold iron bars.

"Back away," he said quietly, "or there will be a bloodbath. I would not wish it, but it will happen if I am pushed. And the blame will solely lie on your shoulders."

Giraud began to sputter, but then, spitting out a most unholy oath, he turned on his heel and stalked out of the barbican.

"Keep going!" William called after him. "Right down to the Market Cross."

When the papal legate had fought his way through crowds of staring, mocking townsfolk, to mount the steps of the battered old cross with its weather-eroded scene of the crucifixion, William ordered his gate sentries to raise the portcullis once more.

Then he motioned to Artois, the captain of the guard, who was pacing around before Giraud's tense retinue, his hand meaningfully planted on his sword hilt. "Artois, see that the legate's men leave in peace."

Artois spoke to Giraud's own captain and staff, presumably telling them their passage to join their master would be safe as long as they behaved themselves.

Hurriedly the leaders mounted their steeds, the ranks formed, the wains were made ready for departure, and then the legate's retinue proceeded towards the palace gatehouse.

After Giraud's men had passed below the jagged dragon's teeth of the portcullis, it clanged down with resounding finality, and the occupants of Poitiers palace all cheered. I breathed a sigh of relief. No blood had been spilt.

William took my arm. "An unpleasant day. I fear my second excommunication is definitely about to take place. But I expected as much. Do not let it trouble you, my dearest—it is time we went for our supper in the hall, and I would not quash your appetite by dwelling on unwholesome thoughts."

"I am worried more about Giraud," I said. "The crowds in the town did not look terribly friendly."

We retreated to the Great Hall and were shortly served a meal of lark's tongues, pickled lampreys, venison haunch and honey-sweetened oatcakes. We endeavoured to pretend nothing was amiss, but before long we were distracted by noise from outside the palace.

Leaving our table, William and I ascended the castle walls, striding along the covered wall-walk past the sentries. Reaching the summit of the gatehouse, just behind the parapet, we gazed down at the crowds gathered below. Red-faced, Giraud the legate was screaming out the words of the Anathema. One of his lackeys was ringing a solemn bell, while Giraud, his hands trembling with rage, slammed shut the Book of Gospels then snatched a lit candle from another flunkey and hurled it on the ground where he trod on it with his shoe. Oh, how I wished it had caught his flying vestments! But no such luck. He finished his nasty little ceremony, glared arrogantly up at the palace walls, and then stomped over to his waiting horse.

The townsfolk catcalled him and a few even threw mouldy cabbages and turnips at his retreating back.

William threw up his hands. "Oh, more trouble. Never mind!"

If one good thing came of William's excommunication, it was the departure of his wife Philippa for the convent of Fontevraud. She had, for reasons unknown, convinced herself that Giraud would succeed in convincing William to send me packing back to Aimery and then beg her on bended knee to return to Poitou.

"I pray she does not continue to scheme against me while in the convent," William said with a sigh. I was lying on a padded couch, shift open to my waist, my hair hanging to the floor in flaming coils. He was painting my image upon his shield; he had some skill as an artist as well as a poet.

"How can she scheme when she is locked away with the nuns?" I popped a grape into my mouth and tried to get a look at how the painting was coming along. It must look right—although the figure he painted was unclad, I must not resemble some wanton trollop, lolling on her bed of sin; instead, I must resemble Venus, that ancient goddess of love, passionate yet powerful and wise.

William harrumphed. "Nuns are the worst schemers. You cannot ever have had many dealings with nunneries, dearest. Even worse, my first wife, Ermengarde of Anjou, is already ensconced at Fontevraud. She has no love of me, alas…and those two harridans cloistered together…"

I sat bolt upright, dropping the grapes. "You were married before Philippa? You did not tell me this."

"Why would you think it necessary to know? It was a long time ago."

"Well… I *am* interested. Tell me about this Ermengarde."

He put down the shield carefully, so as not to smudge his work, and thrust the brushes into a jar of water. Folding his arms, he paced around the room. "Hmm…she was a beautiful girl, sapphire eyes, hair like night. She was educated and charming."

I did not like the sound of that at all but reminded myself that she was long gone.

"However, her moods…my God, Dangereuse. One moment, she would scream at me like a mad harpy; the next she would weep a river of tears for no reason at all. I hardly knew how to speak to her, for whatever I said was wrong and would cause a violent outburst. And she nagged. All day, all night…nag, nag, nag. William, you did not buy me a fancy gown, William, why are you not crusading for God again, William, why have you not immortalised me in song, William, why did you not come to my chamber last night and who was that strumpet I spied you with."

I laughed then, imagining her jealousy. What a foolish woman. She had driven him away. Right from the first, I was clever enough to realise William was never the kind of man to be faithful. Not even to me, although he had not strayed in the time we had spent together—as far as I knew. I did not care where he got extra bed-sports from, as long as I was still foremost in his affections and the others were nought but passing fancies, a quick roll in the hay while he was far from my side.

Leaning against the window shutter, William continued his tale of marital woe. "Whenever we fought, Ermengarde would run to a convent and hide herself away till her temper cooled. Then she would emerge and glide back into my court as if no rift had taken place, expecting praise and adoration. Most of the courtiers thought her moon-mad! After a few years, it became obvious that our marriage would bear no fruit, but she put the blame on me, weeping and wailing about how I had wronged her and shat in the marital bed…She seemed to have forgotten that by that point she would not let me near her, so a baby was unlikely, save through some miracle."

"Silly woman," I said. "Spurning your embraces and avoiding her marital duties. She did not know what she was missing."

He shrugged. "We argued about it constantly. So after one particularly lengthy disagreement, where she trod on my lute and smashed a sitar, I packed her up with her belongings, bundled her into a carriage and sent her back to her father."

"What became of her then? Was her sire angry?"

William shrugged. "I neither know nor care if he was angry. An annulment was obtained and that was that. Her father soon married her off again to Count Alan of Brittany. Alan seemed a little more to her taste, however—she wasn't barren and actually managed to spawn three children. But she was not happy, even so. She kept haranguing Count Alan to let her become a nun, but because she was wed without impediment, no one would allow such a thing. Eventually, though, she got her wish."

"When her husband died?"

"No. I think he'd had enough of her, could not bear her nagging voice any longer. He handed his lands and castles over to his son and became a monk. When this happened, Ermengarde was free to pursue her own dream; she stayed with her eldest boy for a few years to give him guidance, then joined the nuns at Fontevraud. And that is how I have two bitter past wives conspiring against me in that convent."

"I promise I shan't join them," I said stoutly.

"Good. You would make a terrible nun," he said, and then he returned to painting my image on his shield. "This painting is going well, my dearest—I cannot wait to carry it into battle. Then you will lie over me as I have lain over you almost every night since I brought you to Poitiers."

He laughed at his ribald jest, and I smiled and stretched myself out on the couch again, his willing model…yet behind the smile, I was full of deep thought. Could Philippa and Ermentrude cause any further mischief?

As it turned out, Philippa could not. Within six months, word reached Poitiers that she had sickened and died of an ague. "It is wicked but I cannot say I am sorry," said William as we walked in the castle herb gardens in the evening, fresh with the scent of mint and lavender. "She was always trouble!"

Secretly I, too, was glad for I had recently found out I was with child. I did not quite know how I felt about it, as for some silly reason I had believed my childbearing days behind me, which was foolish for I was yet young and William a lusty man. The remembrance of Aenor and Aois' hard birth cast a dark shadow over my mind, but I tried to blot it out.

"We will have to dedicate our child to the church," I said as we strolled amidst blue beds of wild sage, the nodding heads of white Marguerite daisies, the pale pink peonies. The long shadow of the palace's turrets stretched over us, dove-grey and violet. Beyond the walls, the mist was rising, cloaking the streets of Poitiers.

William blinked and halted. "The church? I am surprised to hear you say that."

"A woman with a babe in her belly has many strange fancies," I said, with a wry smile. "But I think on the future. A time must come when we are no longer bright and beautiful, and we must make peace and atonement with God. We can do this by the gift of our child."

I thought he might scorn such sentiment, but his face was solemn. "It is true I have enough children already. If one lives the life of a devil, one must appease God someday, I suppose. Yes...if it is your wish Dangereuse, any fruit born of our union shall enter the House of God. A peace offering, one might say."

At year's end, I gave birth to a fine, healthy boy who we named Henri. He was a round, quiet baby with a fringe of spiky dark hair that already gave him the semblance of a monkish tonsure. He was a joy to his nurses so sweet-tempered was he, and William and I soon decided that he would become a monk at Cluny when he was older. For now, he would live at Poitiers, cared for by the best nursemaids that could be found and then by skilled tutors when he grew older.

William, his mood much sweetened by the birth of his latest son, listened to my pleas and petitioned for absolution and the lifting of his excommunication. This was, to his surprise, granted, with no further reference to my presence at Poitiers. Although not known for piety, I did not want my lover to dwell forever outside the church—especially now that we had a child together. An excommunicated sire might harm Henri's chances in the future.

And soon it was not just one child whose future we had to decide. Another babe followed swiftly after little Henri—a girl we named Sybill. Another child to be gifted to the church, although, I freely admitted, I was a little sorry, for she was pretty, like a sweet poppet.

Sybill was only a few months old when trouble began anew, threatening our happiness.

Ermengarde, William's first wife. Figure of many a jest. Well, neither William nor I were laughing now.

She had taken up the sword, figurately, on the behalf of her dead friend Philippa, and for her own grievances too, it would seem.

Pope Calixtus had convened a Synod to forge a peace with Henry, the Holy Roman Emperor. Fifteen archbishops, two hundred bishops and another two hundred abbots were in attendance—and Ermengarde, leaving Fontevraud's cloister like a fury, burst in upon their meeting, throwing herself down on her knees in front of the startled Pontiff.

If I had been Pope, I would have cast the disrespectful harridan out of the hall, but I suppose Calixtus had to appear somewhat more forgiving than ordinary people, being a holy man and messenger of God. Ermengarde had cried a river of false tears, asking that William be excommunicated for a third time, and I be cast forth from the palace, leaving her to take her 'rightful place' as Duchess of Aquitaine and Countess of Poitou. I swear her mind must have turned from too much time on her knees praying in the abbey—she seemed to have forgotten altogether that William had packed her off to her sire and their marriage had been dissolved, hence her subsequent union with Alan of Brittany. What she was claiming was ludicrous, as it surely would negate her second marriage and make all her children illegitimate...

"She is mad," I said to William. We were sharing a quiet hour in the Maubergeon with little Henri laid upon a fury lambskin between us and Sybill in a cradle near the brazier. "What did she think would happen—that they would start a religious crusade against you?"

He brushed a hand through his hair, grown shaggy over the last few months. Soon we would need the barber to tame those tangled curls! "She certainly acted the part of a moon-calf. And the Pope knew it. He listened to her complaints with nodding head and benign smile, then he dismissed her and told her to seek more contemplation of the divine to give her peace and serenity."

"I'd wager she was not pleased," I said darkly, as I dangled a bead on a string before little Henri's fascinated gaze.

"No, she was not." A frown crossed William's visage. "And there lies the problem. One would have thought she would have sought the sisters in Fontevraud once her plea had been rejected by His Holiness. But no, it is reported she left the synod with a face black as thunder and rode for Toulouse."

"Toulouse?"

He frowned and his fingers drummed against the bench on which he sat; something he did when nervous or peeved. "I sent my spies to track her movements as any sensible fellow would do in such circumstances. She had sought out my son William's castle in Toulouse. He liked me ill enough before, but now Ermengarde foments pure hatred in his heart, telling him how much his mother had suffered from my abuse. How it contributed to her demise."

A little slither of breath emerged between my teeth. Little Willy was not so little anymore. He had inherited Toulouse since Philippa had been the sole heir to her late father, but naturally, he would want his paternal inheritance one day too—and with a grievance against his sire, he might decide he wanted it sooner rather than later.

"Do you think he will do anything rash?"

William shrugged. "Maybe. He is impetuous, as I was at his age. We will just have to see, Dangereuse. But do not fear, my men are more numerous than any he might muster, and although our abode is a palace of pleasure as much as any war-castle, its walls are thick and its gates secure."

Sybill began to wail, a thin, high sound that set my teeth on edge. I picked her up from her cradle, jiggling her to soothe her gripes.

By the Rood, I hoped William was right and that overgrown pup, Little Willy, was not preparing to show us the sharpness of his new-grown teeth.

CHAPTER TEN

Young William gathered his pitiful army outside of the walls of Poitiers. Ermengarde was at his side, dressed in nun-like raiment yet pretending she was some kind of ancient warrior Queen, striding about in front of the troops while she shouted that God had summoned her to punish her errant former husband.

William had ordered the town gates shut and every archer to man the walls. Watchfires flickered throughout the long night, filling the air with spark and the acrid scent of burning. Occasionally, the inexperienced Willy would make a frontal assault on the gates with much chaos and noise, and the soldiers above would throw down buckets of pig swill and their own piss to cool his juvenile ardour. Once they had even hurled some rotten fruit that landed in a deep piss-puddle and sent up a rancid yellow wave which spoiled the nunly robes of Lady Ermengarde. She had emitted some very un-Christian curses and stormed back to her pavilion.

As time dragged on and Little Willy showed no signs of moving on, William did begin to become a little concerned. "We are well supplied, but our stores will not last forever. Already there is rationing and unrest in the town. The people cannot go about their business, nor can I—my own revenues are rapidly diminishing. I must put a stop to this folly." He smacked his clenched right fist into the palm of his left hand.

I jumped in alarm at the sharpness of the sound. I did not want him to enjoin in battle with Willy; fights between fathers and sons could often turn out tragic for all concerned. "I beg you, wait a little longer. He cannot breach the town walls; we have seen that. He has no engines, only a handful of grappling hooks. He will eventually give up, surely."

William shook his head. His expression was more serious than I had ever seen it. "I fear William might go to my enemies and make alliances with them. If too many join his banner, the situation becomes grave. Other lords have greater experience of war—they may bring sappers to undermine the town walls or know how to poison the town well. In particular—I think of your husband, Count Aimery. He has no cause to love me."

"My *husband*? Do not call him that!" I spat. "I no longer think of him as my husband—indeed, I rarely think of him at all."

"But I would wager he thinks of you, Dangereuse. You hurt his pride in the worst possible way. He fears other men laughing at him—and they do. Joining with young William might be, in his mind, a way to win new prestige…and to get you back."

"Get me back!" I cried, furiously indignant. Jesu, I could hardly remember Aimery's face these days, he meant so little to me.

"He has never sought an annulment, has he? Or publicly brought forth a mistress to replace you. And why would he? You, my sweetling, are irreplaceable."

"At this moment, I wish Aimery had chased the skirts of a thousand trulls and forgot I ever existed," I said. "What is your counsel, William?"

"I must stop young Will before this siege becomes too serious. If I have to kill him, I will. I have other sons. Raymond, my second boy, bears me less ill will."

I heard the grief raw in his voice and shivered. "I pray it will not come to killing."

He nodded. "I wish it too, but it is in God's hands."

"When will you make your move?" My heart was beating strongly, pounding against the enclosure of my ribs.

"As soon as possible. I want this to be over, one way or another."

"William...will you be in danger?"

"I am a Crusader. I lived for danger then! This latest exploit won't be without risk, I am certain...but I will endeavour to return to you in one piece."

I put my hands to my face. "William...William...Let me come with you. Maybe I could parlay with Ermengarde. Woman speaking to woman."

He shook his head, placing his hands firmly on my shoulders. "No, my fierce little Amazon. I know you have a man's heart but I will not risk any harm coming to you. If it makes you feel better, I plan to try to avoid a fatal confrontation as best I can, using something better than a sword."

"And what is that?"

"My brain." He tapped the side of his skull with a ringed finger. "I would prefer to capture him, not slay him."

All nerves, I waited on the Maubergeon's top floor, sewing distractedly to keep my hands busy. When daylight failed, my maids went about lighting cressets; I paid them little attention. Where was William now? Had he met with his son? Was he safe—or was he being dragged off in chains...or worse? One girl asked if I wanted a platter from the kitchen. I shook my head and dismissed her; my stomach was sour, churning with my fear. I had a bowl of sops earlier—wine mixed with bread; that would suffice.

Throwing down my stitchery, which was full of ragged mistakes, I pulled on my cloak and sought the tiny staircase leading to the top of the turret. The Mauburgeon was the tallest of all the towers in the palace, guarded by two solitary bowmen gathered around a brazier whose flames fluttered in the wind of the height. Both men bowed as I approached.

Ignoring them, I went over to the crenellations and leaned forward, staring out beyond the palace walls and then the town walls, alight with watchfires to match those on the top of the palace towers. Distantly, through the night haze, I could see the enemy encampment—tents and campfire and moving men and horses. Although William had assured me that they were not that great in number, it seemed like thousands assembled before the walls, as many as the stars in the hard black arch of the sky above. Brought on the wind, I heard the ringing of horse harness, the shouts of captains calling orders, a chorus of drunken singing. I felt very alone, and for the first time, afraid, and even a little guilty—I was, in great part, responsible for the woes that had befallen my lover.

*If he never returned...*I wandered back to my apartments. I freed the maids of their duties and sat in silence, the cressets extinguished, only one solitary lighted taper giving me light. Eventually, I lay down upon the bed, upon the very sheets where I had lain with William the previous night. Filled with melancholy, I wondered if that had been the last time, and wondered what I would do if evil befell him. I could not stay in Poitiers; I would have to leave before I was cast out. I refused to return to Aimery. My parents both still lived, but I doubted they would want me back after the shame I had brought with the desertion of my husband…

I might have to seek a convent for sanctuary, somewhere far away where no one would recognise my face or know my reputation. Rare tears prickled at my eyelids; I had not thought it might come to this. That the singing and dancing and poetry, the decadent nights and splendorous days riding out with all pageantry, might one day end abruptly and in tragedy.

After some hours, I sank into a restless sleep, lying sprawled on these sheets that still bore the scent, the imprint of my lover. I woke to the sound of the Lauds bell ringing softly from the town church. It was early morning before the sun had risen, and the room was ice-cold, the candle a puddle of hardened wax.

Outside, far below, I thought I heard a noise, faint, indistinct. A chill ran up my spine. I knew it was William…*I knew*.

Pulling on my shoes, I stumbled down the stairs and out through the door into the lightening darkness. The postern gate…Just as I had slipped in and out of the postern gate at Châtellerault, William was returning through the one at Poitou.

Breath bursting out in a white cloud, I raced through the gloomy gardens, rose thorns ripping my dress, tree boughs snatching at my hair. Before me, loomed the postern gateway. There were already soldiers waiting, shadowed, unlit by any torchlight. I stood still, the chill of the earth below me running up my legs like the chill of the grave as the cast iron gate ground open.

In marched William, unhurt and very much alive; relief made my knees grow weak. He looked smug, and a moment later, I saw why. Two prisoners bound and gagged were being hustled towards the confines of the castle. One was Little Willy, his eyes wild and furious above the gag, his cheeks mottled red as he struggled against his bonds; the other I surmised was Ermengarde, who was more restrained in her actions but whose eyes blazed with hatred.

William signalled for a captain. "Take this pair of rebels to cool down in the cellars. Inform them that they will be thrown into a real dungeon with chains and rats if they do not cease to strive against me. Keep them away from my wine stores, mind—there's little enough left in the cellars."

Ermengarde now began to struggle as much as Little Willy, her strident yells muffled by the thick gag. William turned his face away, ignoring her protests.

He saw me standing there, dishevelled and still breathing heavily, and he smiled and extended his mailed hand. "Come, Dangereuse, I want to get out of my armour."

In William's apartments, I sat on a quilted stool while my lover's squire removed his mail coat and then the gambeson beneath.

"So, how did this miracle occur?" I asked as another squire dressed William and a third brought a bowl of water and cloths to wash his face and hands. "And there I was, half-crazed with fear, believing you slain by Ermengarde's jealous hand."

William laughed, rubbing at his wet face with the cloth. "I know Will's weaknesses…and Ermengarde's. I managed to arrange negotiations by playing the part of a sorrowing father, sore-wounded by his son's actions but admitting his own flaws, as well as a poor husband willing to make amends to a woman wronged."

I arched an eyebrow. "So you lied to them to make you think you were repentant…and weak."

"Of course! I told the pair of them that you were, er, leaving…"

"William!" A jolt of anger and dismay struck through me, along with a little fear. I did not like to hear such sentiments, even in jest. Who knew what was in the heart of my womanising beloved?

He reached out and drew me to him. He had not shaved in a few days; his stubble was harsh against my cheek. "Do not fret, my dearest. Another lie that the pair of them swallowed. Ermengarde is a vain woman, and she fell for my tale of how I realised, by her faithfulness to my son's cause, that she was fit to return as my true wife. Filled with such mad hope, she begged Will to cease all hostilities; she feared that if he continued to war against me, I might be slain or deposed and her plans for her own elevation would lie in ruins. With both me and Ermengarde working on the boy, he agreed to lay down his arms and become a dutiful son once more, with Ermengarde restored to her former status as Duchess of Aquitaine. I asked them to join me in a Mass of celebration in one of our churches. By this time, they had become sloppy, careless and maudlin—I had made sure they both had downed copious quantities of celebratory wine!"

I burst into laughter. "So *that's* why you mentioned the wine in our cellars and Ermengarde grew so enraged!"

Grinning, he nodded. "It was dusk when they stumbled up to the church. They had brought a few guards, which they were persuaded to leave outside. Once we had entered the nave, my own men, in greater numbers, overpowered these fellows with little bloodshed required. Will's soldiers were not very enthusiastic anyway, as they were all aware that he is not yet of age and acting the fool, thus endangering their lives. Most laid down their arms willingly."

I put my hands on my knees. "When did they find out their plans were undone?"

"I had a false priest waiting inside the church. He asked us all to kneel. As we did, my men ran out of the clerestory and vestry and took hold of William and Ermengarde. So I had my dear son and former wife trussed up like lambs to the slaughter and carried to the palace in secret."

"What do you plan to do with them now? They cannot stay in the cellar forever."

"With Will's army dispersed, we will now begin proper negotiations for a true peace. I will get what I want, and they will get…their freedom."

"I want to sit in on these talks," I said. "I want them both to understand that you will never cast me forth on the say-so of either of them—or anyone else."

Leaning forward, he kissed me lightly on the mouth, his kiss full of the promise of more later on, when he had sufficiently rested. I smelt the smoke of the campfires in his hair, tasted salt upon his lips, and it was wondrous. "So be it, my lady. You shall sit at my side, my eternal Queen of Love."

I smiled, stroking his cheek with my fingertip. "But before we begin to negotiate, I must discuss something else with you. I have an idea that might keep young William at bay, and also, should he ever become troublesome, my former husband Aimery."

"Do tell?"

"Later," I said. "In bed. I have missed you and worried about you and want you close to me. It is also a good place to make plans. And other things."

"Indeed it is." His eyes sparkled, full of admiration…and anticipation.

The prisoners were brought into the Great Hall three days later—William wanted them to have plenty of time in the dim, damp cellar to contemplate their misdeeds. My lover and I reclined on throne-like chairs upon the dais, under a canopy of Italian silk as radiant as the sun. William wore his ducal coronet and rich robes; I wore a striking green bliaut and my hair was netted in a mesh of gold and pearls. I had applied cosmetics with the aid of my maids, which included imported kohl to darken the brows and eyelids, giving a sultry, unconventional appearance. With gold bangles upon my wrists and a silver-star necklace appended by a rock crystal, I probably resembled some exotic eastern Queen, a dangerous incarnation of Jezebel or Delilah perhaps. Exactly the appearance I wanted.

Little Willy looked pasty and sullen, his shirt sweat-stained and his hair matted with straw. Ermengarde, surprisingly, was more defiant than the boy, her arms folded defensively over her rumpled gown. Her feelings had been toyed with, and she was still angry she had succumbed to William's blandishments. Angry with herself as well as him.

William cleared his throat. "I plan to set you free today, but first you must swear on your knees that you will never attack me or mine again. Remember, William, I have a younger son, your brother Raymond; if you continue to defy me, I can have you disinherited, although it would pain me to do so. Ermengarde, I want you to swear you will retire in peace to Fontevraud and never bother me more."

The scorned wife stumbled forward, snarling and spitting like an affronted cat; the guards crossed their spears in front of her face in alarm. She cared not a jot, staring crazy-eyed between the sharpened blades. "You lied to me, William. That is all you've ever done. Lie…And all for the indecent harlot you parade on the dais in place of a proper wife."

"You seemed to prefer nuns' company to that of your husband," I said calmly. "Perhaps *that* was the issue with your marriage, Lady."

Ermengarde sputtered and looked even more furious, if that were possible, her fists curling into impotent fists at her side. "You…you…" she sputtered, spittle on her lips…

And then, quite unexpectedly, she burst into tears. She cowered back, covering her face with her hands. "How did I come to this pass? Why did I get involved in this madness?" she moaned, rocking from side to side. "I do not know what has possessed me…it must be a demon of pride and sinfulness! Oh God, forgive me!"

She fell to the floor, weeping, ugly in her anguish. Little Willy stared with a look of complete disgust. I thought he might kick her and motioned the guards to move him away.

Ermengarde continued to jabber madly, half to herself, it seemed, but perhaps also to me. "I never truly wanted to live as William's wife again, enduring all the embarrassments and heartbreak he put me through. I was moved by Philippa's plight when she came to Fontevraud, and I took on her woes as my own. I felt if I forced William to take me back, vengeance would be wreaked in both our names…" She collapsed on her side, hugging herself with her arms. "My head was all afire with mad thoughts…I scorned the kind nuns who try to aid me and joined a treacherous son on a fool's mission. I should be flogged with willow withies to atone…until the blood comes!"

William glanced solemnly over at me as Ermengarde continued to writhe and wail. "I told you her moods were volatile." He tapped his skull. "I have always believed she was moonstruck rather than malicious."

I rose and approached the other woman. She had torn off her wimple; brown hair streaked with grey tumbled down to trail in the trampled rushes on the floor. "Calm yourself, Ermengarde," I said.

She glanced up at me in mingled confusion and hatred.

"I am not your enemy, no matter what you may think," I told her. "You are daughter to a great lord; you have had two powerful husbands…remember your dignity."

I stretched out a hand towards her. She hesitated, and then, with a grimace, grabbed hold of it. I hauled her to her feet; she stood before me, wavering. "There," I said, "we stand as equals. Do you admit your folly in this endeavour, and to return to your cloistered life anon?"

Her mouth was sour but she nodded vigorously. "I do. Now that my mind is clear again, I want nothing more than to return to the cloisters of Fontevraud." She tilted her head up, and her eyes glittered, filled with tears and despair. "After meeting my first husband anew, I realised why I despised him all those years ago. All his false flattery, his effete poets…his loose women…"

I supposed she referred to me with her last jibe, but I refused to rise to the bait and smiled sweetly. Cloyingly. "Farewell then, Lady Ermengarde," I said. "I am sorry the circumstances of our first and hopefully only encounter were such strange, unsavoury ones. It would be best if you never set foot in Poitiers again; his Grace the Duke will never change to the bloodless creature you desire, and I will always be here sharing both his board and his bed."

I stood back, and William beckoned to a couple of guards. "Have Lady Ermengarde put in a chariot and escorted to the Abbey of Fontevraud. Make sure she does not try to escape while on the road...although I think she has had a hard lesson and will not try such foolishness again. Tell the Abbess, the Venerable Petronilla, that I want her watched closely—and I am even willing to pay for such surveillance. Money is one of the favourite things of the Abbess, I am sure, like most of her kind. Collecting for Christ."

"You are so...*disrespectful*." Ermengarde cast him a daggered glare. "Age has not changed you—you are worse than I remember! Fear not, I shall not return."

Ermengarde shuffled around, turning her back to the dais to show her disdain, and beckoned to the waiting guards as if they were her servants rather than William's. "Come on, then. Show me to my carriage. I am more than ready to leave this lowly house of infamy!"

She flounced from the room in a circle of spears, as William tried to keep a solemn demeanour and hide the smirk pulling at the corner of his mouth.

I returned to my seat and William regained his dignified composure. "Now," he said, "I deal with my errant son." Stern as stone, he gazed down from the dais at spotty Little Willy. "What have you to say for yourself, William? I never expected my own child would turn traitor! Do you know what the punishment would be for any other, save you?"

Willy shuffled uncomfortably. Beads of sweat gathered, glistening, on his brow.

"Cat got your tongue, *son*? I'll tell you...shall I? I'd have then stripped and torn apart by four galloping horses, then put the quarters of their bodies on the gates of Poitiers, Toulouse and Bordeaux. You will escape such punishment this time...but I will be less lenient should it happen again."

"You disgraced my mother!" Willy suddenly blurted. "What kind of son would I be if I did not protect my mother?"

"She coddled you too much."

"Well, *you* ignored me. You always preferred Raymond!"

"Well, that should be no surprise. He is an intelligent youth who shares interests with me, his father."

Little Willy looked almost apoplectic. "You would say that, wouldn't you? Raymond has always been a lickarse, running after you like a dog, pretending to admire your bloody troubadours!"

"Well, you, Will...you seemed to like or appreciate nothing. You're like your mother."

"You slander her again!" yelled Will, eyes wild. "And me! I-I am educated, I am just less *prurient* than you!"

I reached over and grasped William's hand. I did not think he should rile Little Willy further, lest the lad explode in rage again and do something regretted by all.

My calming motion, however, did not have the desired effect on Will. His arm lifted; his shaking finger pointed. "Although you always were like a dog in heat where sluts were concerned, never before did you take up with one before...that...that creature! You moved her into your house! In the end, I swear to God, it killed my mother! You are accountable for her death and you should pay..."

He lunged forward, slipping under the tips of the guard's spears, as slippery as an eel, and flung himself at

William with his hands stretching for his throat and a murderous light in his eyes.

William uttered a mighty roar of rage and sprang to his feet, diving to meet Little Willy's headlong rush. A moment later the boy lay on the steps of the dais, his lip bleeding, his chest heaving with gasping breaths. William knelt at his side, his elbow firmly pressed across his windpipe. "Yield, young whelp...*yield*!" he ordered.

"I—I yield!" gasped young Will, his cheeks flame-red, his eyes bulging with the veins like streaks of fire.

I stood up, gazing upon the two of them on the floor. "Young William, this hatred for me must be put to bed for once and for all. And 'bed' is the very best way to end it."

He struggled into a sitting position, his mouth gawping like an idiot's. "You want to *sleep* with me?"

"Do not be ridiculous." I folded my arms. "But we are to become as one. One family. You, dear Will, are going to marry my daughter."

CHAPTER ELEVEN

"You want me to marry *who*?"

I stood before my daughter, Aenor, within her chamber in the castle of Châtellerault. I had not seen her for some years and she was now a woman grown, dark-tressed like her father and beautiful, with long gleaming hair and deep, leaf-green eyes. She should have been contracted for marriage long ago, but her father Aimery had seemed reluctant to find a match. Aois had entered a convent and Amabel was wed to Wulgrin of Angouleme. Raoul was contracted to Lady Elizabeth of Faye-la-Vineuse. Only Hugh, our eldest and Aimeri's heir, was as yet still unwed—I thought this foolish at his age, but no doubt his sire was hoping for a spectacular match and unwilling to commit him too soon.

"William, eldest son of the Duke of Aquitaine. The heir to the Duchy. A fine match!"

Aenor stomped her foot. "Mother! Marrying the son of my mother's lover? People will gossip; people will laugh. No, I shan't have it!"

"I have spoken to your father. He agrees it is a good match."

My meeting with Aimery had been a fraught occasion, with my former husband eyeing me suspiciously as if he thought I might stab him with a secreted dagger and take his castle for myself. He had grown very unkempt and prematurely grey, the handsomeness of youth completely fled, while I had matured but retained a good deal of my attractiveness. I had expected him to heap harsh words upon me but he had stayed quiet and startlingly business-like. He was not a complete fool after all. He knew the offer of this marriage was a profitable one for all. "I will agree to this union," he said, "but only if Aenor also agrees upon it. I would not have her forced into any marriage, and truth be told, I quite enjoy her presence here. She looks after me and runs the household. She has almost taken on the role of Lady of Châtellerault—after you abandoned it."

I began to walk around Aenor's room, picking up her trinkets, her combs, her jewels. Most of them looked tawdry to me, childish and cheap. She deserved more. "Listen, Aenor, you are unlikely to get another opportunity to become a Duchess. The marriage would also help your father's stature. Châtellerault and all its furnishings are s so…so aged and tasteless compare to those in the Palace at Poitou. You should see it, Aenor—vast towers filled with exotic silks and spices, sunken baths, imported wines and fruits, handsome troubadours and poets everywhere, strolling about in gardens that are almost as fair as…as Eden."

"If I am wed, my eyes will not be fixed on comely singers and poets," she said fiercely. "I am not that sort of woman." Unspoken words hung between us—"*unlike you*".

I sighed, a little defensive. "Oh, Aenor, I can tell you are still cross with me for the events of the past, but you are no longer a child. You must forget about what happened years ago, and think of your future."

Her lips parted and for a moment I thought she would subject me to a bitter tirade, but then she folded her arms and fixed me with a straightforward stare. "I would like to be a Duchess, that much is true. If I am to be given to a man like a prize cow, I may as well get something to enjoy in return—wealth, prestige, silks, castles. Tell me, then, what is this William the Younger like?"

I licked my lips. I had best not tell her I called him 'Little Willy.' "He has grown tall, very tall, beyond most other men—surely an admirable quality. He is a bit…pimpled …but such blemishes usually vanish with age. His hair is brown, not so dark as your own, and thick and wavy. His features are regular, his teeth are white and good—no one has knocked them out yet, anyway—he bathes and changes his raiment frequently, and his father saw that he was well-educated."

"What is he like with women?" she said suspiciously. "I realise men often take their pleasure where they will but…" her green eyes narrowed beneath their fringe of long black lashes, "some men are worse than others in that regard, always chasing other's men's wives. His father the current Duke is the prime example."

Her words were another stab at me, but I ignored her petty jibe. I was well-armoured against such sharp arrows of spite nowadays. "Young Will is of a quite different temperament to his father. He appears to be more abstemious where women are concerned. He spent much time with his mother, Philippa, and they were close. From what I have seen, he is not a chaser of skirts or a haunter of brothels. Indeed, I have never seen him in any kind of entanglement with a girl."

"That may not entirely be a good thing either," sniffed Aenor, hands now drifting to her hips. "He may be all horses and hounds and dull sporting pursuit…or…he might even like…boys!" She began to pace, her long skirts swishing, her dark braid swinging like a lion's tail. "Oh, yes, I'm not ignorant. I know of such things…"

"I am sure you do," I said dryly. I was sure she really knew very little, even if she believed otherwise, but she clearly wanted to appear hard and worldly, able to bargain for the terms of her own marriage. "I do not believe William is that way inclined either."

"I would not put up with such an affront!" she warned.

I flung up my hands and rolled my eyes. "I am sure if worst came to worst and you despised each other at first sight, the marriage could be set aside without consummation and no harm done. Now, come, daughter, you are making this long-winded and difficult. I do not have all day, and my feet grow weary. Will you take William of Aquitaine as your husband or not?"

She paused, hesitating, face unreadable, no doubt deliberately making me wait for her answer. Then she nodded curtly. "You will nag me, I'm sure, if I do not. Yes…yes, I will marry William the Younger and become Duchess of Aquitaine one day."

So Aenor was wed to Little Willy, whom I now endeavoured to call merely 'Will', out of politeness since I was now his mother-by-marriage. To my relief, the young couple seemed happier than I had expected, knowing my daughter's fears and her husband's shortcomings. Grudgingly, I had to admit that Will was maturing and losing many of the foibles that had made him so despicable a few years back. The newlyweds had comfortable quarters within the main Palace, while I still resided in the opulence of Maubergeon, so I saw them often and would embroider with my daughter or sit with her to listen to the poets.

It was lonely though, despite having my daughter in Poitiers. William had gone on campaign in Spain in 1120, joining forces with the Kings of Leon and Castile to take the city of Cordoba from the Moslem rulers. He had not even waited for Aenor and Will's marriage to take place. I had railed at him about travelling so far afield at his age, but he had rebuked me more sternly than ever before in all the time we had spent together. "Philippa's dower lands were recently lost to Alfonso Jourdain, whose father Raymond was always after Philippa's lands, so my son has lost a large portion of his inheritance. I feel guilty for allowing Alfonso to take over so easily—therefore I shall expiate that guilt by fighting against the paynim and returning Cordoba to Christendom."

"Will does not appear to care too much about the loss of Toulouse and his mother's lands," I had said, clinging to his sleeve, trying to keep him with me, away from distant wars that meant little to me. His crusading days needed to lie in the past. "For him, Aquitaine with its fine towns and castles is the prize. If you are so concerned, why not raise forces against Alfonso Jourdain, instead of embarking on this mad crusade in faraway lands?"

"Alfonso is Count of Rouergue, and claimant for Provence and Narbonne, as well as Toulouse," said William. "He thinks he is specially designated by God to rule because he was baptised in the River Jordan. He is determined to assert his rights."

"What about Will's rights?" I could not believe I was defending Little Willy.

"You said it yourself, my sweeting. He is not much bothered about Toulouse. He does not want to see the blood of good Christians spilt and cousins drawn into conflict, and neither do I. Many, too, believe Alfonso *is* the rightful heir to Toulouse, which could prove problematic."

"Well, why go to war at all then, holy or otherwise? Why do you feel guilty if you know that Will hardly cares?"

He sighed and suddenly he looked old, lines creeping like dark dreams under his eyes. "I feel I have failed William sometimes—as a father, as his Lord. We lack a closeness even now. And I am growing into an old man, and I mull on all my sins. God has spoken to me—wanting me to make amends."

"God has spoken to me." I doubted that very much; more like it was the restiveness older men often felt, an urge to prove they are still brave and hardy, that dotage and the grave were still many, many years in the future

Whatever was in William's troubled head, he left me for the first time in all our years together, riding towards Spain surrounded by a large contingent of men with banners raised and horns blaring.

I was not a woman who wept much, but as his host vanished into the hazy distance, I went into the Maubergeon and wept where none could witness it. The happiness I'd known for so long faded as a leaf is touched by frost and withers, and the glories of the palace became dull and tarnished, the songs unbearable, the poets vapid and shallow. It was hot in Poitou that year and the wine withered and grapes fell, splattering on paving tiles where flies and wasps gathered, buzzing like insects around carrion.

Will and Aenor continued on as if nothing had changed, holding first their lavish wedding celebration, then continuing with great feasts and tourneys and hunts. They acted as if they already ruled Poitou and Aquitaine, as if they believed William would never return from his quest....while I stayed within the cool walls of the Maubergeon, waiting and praying for news from the south. Maybe this would be my punishment for being an untrue wife...maybe William would be lost to me, not to the arms of another woman, but to the arms of death. The very thought almost ripped the breath from my own body, making me feel weak at knees and ill.

My sorrow was ameliorated, however, when Aenor sought me in the tower to tell me she was with child. She glowed with the news; she had not been married long and already showed that she was fertile. We held a special mass of thanks in the palace chapel, and Will threw a banquet for all the nobles far and wide. He prayed the infant would be a lusty boy, heir to Poitou and Aquitaine.

"I am sure it will be a boy," said Aenor with confidence, some months later, running her hands over the growing swell of her belly. "The babe is not quiet, as I would expect a girl to be. It kicks nearly all the time; a little warrior waiting desperately to enter the world."

But when the child arrived in the month of April the following year, taking the first breath of life when the trees were newly blooming and birds darting against azure skies, it was a little girl who burst screaming into this wicked world, her strong voice echoing around the confines of the palace.

"God's Teeth, that child has a set of lungs on her!" exclaimed Will when the news was brought to the Great Hall "I hope she will not howl so at her future husband!"

He feigned displeasure that the infant was female, but his face was beaming when she was brought to him so that he could acknowledge her. He was disappointed the babe was not male, of course, but not overly concerned. Aenor had quickened so fast, the young Duke was certain that she would produce at least a dozen more babies in short order.

I entered my daughter's birthing chamber, locked fast against the world and stifling hot. She lay abed, face drained but satisfied. A nursemaid carried in the swaddled child from Will's solar and laid her in Aenor's arms. She rocked the child gently.

I peered at the red, yelling face and gradually the infant began to quiet. No newborn baby is particularly pretty if one is honest—comeliness comes later to a child—but this one had a special quality, a promise of beauty. Her hair was dark like Aenor's, but the shape of her jaw and brows and eyes were mine. One day, I mused, she would be fair indeed. I hoped such looks would prove a boon and not a curse.

"Have you and William decided on a name for her?" I asked.

"Yes," she said. "She will be Christened Alienor...*Alia Aenor,* the other Aenor."

I crowed with laughter; I had not thought my daughter so clever as to devise such a name.

"Do you not like the name, mother?" Aenor frowned

"I actually like it very much," I told her. "I would never have expected you to call her something unwieldy...like Amauberge! The name would be Eleanor in the *langues d'oil,* which is also fair on the ear."

"She should have been a boy, though," said Aenor sadly. "I was so sure."

"You will have more children," I said confidently.

The baby began to fret again. I took her from my weary daughter and walked around the lying-in chamber, staring down into that extraordinary, wailing, demanding, entrancing face.

Eleanor. Eleanor of Aquitaine.

News arrived from Spain, brought by a much-delayed courier on a weary horse. A battle had been fought, in a place called Cutanda. William and his men, alongside his allies' armies from Navarre and Aragon, were victorious against the troops of the Almoravid Emir, Ali Ibn Yusuf. God smiled upon their efforts against the infidel, and the enemy army was crushed and their greatest captain slain. However, William was not returning yet. The Spanish Kings hoped to press their advantage home, and capture many fortified towns.

But at least I knew, for the moment, that my beloved was alive and well. Relief filled me like a rush of cool water.

More pleasing news followed. Aenor became with child within months after Eleanor's birth and soon produced another girl-child. This time, Aenor and William quarrelled about the name, my daughter favouring Petronilla and Will insisting on Aelith. I mediated between the warring couple, who had come close to blows, and said that the child must learn she had two names and she could choose the one she preferred when she was older. For now, she would use Petronilla.

In the autumn of 1123, when the summer heat had passed and the forests and fields outside Poitiers began to turn jewel red, burnt umber and faded gold,   William returned from his victorious Spanish campaign, marching down the road to the town gates as if he had merely been out on an afternoon's jaunt.

He entered the palace grounds and dismounted his destrier in the bailey. His armour was dull, hazed with dust; faded and torn banners hung limp in the hands of the standard-bearers. He yanked off his conical helm, dinted and scratched revealing his shaggy, sun-bleached hair and an untrimmed beard that made him look older than his years.

Like some silly maiden, I ran to his stirrup, unable to help myself. I must have looked a sight, my wimple askew, my hair trailing out, coils of fire down the bodice of my smock. I could imagine all the whispering going on behind various hands...but I cared nothing for gossip. Never had, never would.

William laughed, his teeth shining white against that unsightly beard and his sun-browned face, and pulled me up before him on his saddle. He rode around the bailey with me sitting high before him, and the household cheered and roared its approval. Even young Will, who had disliked me so much in the early days managed to keep from looking like he'd sucked a lemon—although that may have been because my daughter Aenor was standing at his side.

Later, a feast of celebration and thanksgiving for William's triumphant homecoming was held—with a *brewet* of capons, and chicken drenched in an amazing azure sauce made from blackberries mixed with verjuice, almonds and ginger. During the final course, when the pastries and honey cakes were served, Aenor and Will's children were brought in to meet and get the blessing of their grandfather.

He stared entranced at little Eleanor, as most folk seemed to when they saw her, both men and women, youngsters and elders alike. Little enchantress, even at that young age. Of course, as it stood, she was young Will's heir presumptive, which made her a Very Important little girl...and a prospective prize to many men wishing to up their station in life.

Later, after William had been shaved and shorn and bathed in the huge wooden tub with its silk canopy, he and I feasted again—but not on meat, though the damson wine ran free in our goblets, over our hot bare skin.

In the aftermath, he had his servants bring in gifts he had purchased in Spain—silks and Castilian gold, pomegranates and raisins, flagons of olive oil, glass lanterns in fabulous colours.

"You should have seen Cordoba," he said, as he held up one lit lantern, its colours flaring out in prismed patterns across the chamber. "I must say, the infidels are great builders and their cities cannot be rivalled by any in Christendom, save perhaps Constantinople or Rome. They have not just fine palaces, with beautiful stonework and domes, but dozens of water conduits in their towns, fountains and parks with trees to shelter one from the heat of the sun. Do not tell anyone I gave their works such praise, Dangereuse—some might question my loyalty and my Faith when all I truly want to do is give praise where it is due."

"My lips are sealed," I assured him. "I wish I could have seen these sights too."

"Not all Moslems are bad fellows," he said. "I learnt that long ago in the Holy Land. In Spain, we even had a Moslem ally, Emir Imad-al-dawla of Saragossa. He gave me a fine gift as a token of friendship—I am minded to gift it in turn to my little granddaughter, Eleanor."

"Oh," I reclined on amber silk, a cushion with tassels at my head, as I ate a sugar-dipped fig. "I am intrigued. What is it?"

William called for a servant. A cedar wood box with silver hinges was carried in and placed carefully on the floor. William flipped back the lid with a clatter, revealing a vase of rock crystal. He turned it in his hands—shaped like a pear, the crystal glass was carved to resemble the honeycomb in a beehive. I had never seen the like before.

"It is very ancient," he said, "the glass has come from the Eastern Mediterranean. Perhaps four hundred years old."

"It is beautiful." I took the vase from him and let my fingertips drift over the bumpy honeycomb pattern. "Do you think it is true what they say—that crystal is petrified ice?"

"It must be," he said. "What else could it be?"

"It will be a fine gift for Eleanor. I am sure Aenor will be pleased. Now let us put it away. I need you. There is so much we must talk about after so long apart."

"Indeed," William smiled. "I wrote a poem for you, Dangereuse...when I sat in my tent at night and thought about your beauty, your passion:

Every joy abases itself,
and every might obeys
the presence of my Mistress,
for the sweetness of her welcome,
for the beauty of her gentle look;
a man who wins the joy of her love
shall live a hundred years."

"Live a hundred years," I murmured. "Oh, God, William, I wish it could be so."

CHAPTER TWELVE

A hundred years of life is not granted to mere sinful mortals, alas. Gone are the days of the Patriarchs of the Bible who lived many centuries. William died in the year of Our Lord 1127—not in battle, not in noble pursuits, not even in my arms engaged in lustful sport...but of a sudden ague that took him swiftly and suddenly. One night with fever and aches, the next day insensible, the day following claimed by death. Gone were the poets, gone the lutanists...the players wore mourning clothes and wept bitter tears, yet they still filed from the palace gates to find new patrons. All the household wore black raiment; voices were hushed and sorrowful.

The palace was like a tomb.

I felt as if I were a tree, its roots slashed asunder, making me unsteady and like to fall. The Maubergeon Tower had been my home for years; now, with young Will as lord, I was nothing but a guest. I wondered how the new Duke would treat me, remembering his mother Philippa and how he had felt about me in the past.

I went to Aenor to voice my fears and woes. We had grown a little closer in the last few years, thanks to dwelling in close proximity to each other, but we had not the love between us of some mothers and daughters. Which was understandable. Bereft, I began to think of my failings as wife and mother, and to feel something I had never felt before—regret.

Aenor and I sat together in the palace arbour. The girls, Eleanor and Petronilla, hopped around in the herb beds, crushing lavender, chewing mint stalks, Eleanor picking up worms to dangle over her sister's head and send her screaming to her nurse. Under a spreading lime tree, a maid sat with the youngest of Aenor's children—William Aigret—wrapped in a blanket. I was glad at least that William had lived long enough to see his grandson born and know the inheritance of Aquitaine was secure.

"Aenor," I said, as I sipped upon sherbet, a cool drink devised by the Moslems which was flavoured by pomegranate, orange blossom and cherries, "what do you think I should do? Is it fitting that I remain here in Poitiers?"

She laughed, but her voice sounded a little strained. "When have you ever needed to ask anyone's opinions, Mother? You have always done as you pleased."

"I would stay here, and watch my grandchildren grow…but I understand the world has changed. William, my protector, is dead. Young Will has no cause to love me. I would not come between you and your husband."

She pursed her lips. "You won't." It was not said in a pleasant manner; she meant that no matter what, she would side with William, even if it meant throwing me into the streets. "But perhaps you should think of your future. Did you not inherit lands from your father, my grandsire Bartelmy? He died several years ago."

For the first time, I felt a complete stranger in Poitiers. An unwelcome stranger. "Yes, yes, a few. As he had no sons, most of his possessions went to his brother, my uncle. They were meant to be mine but he took them as is often the way…and I had none to battle for them."

She blinked. "No help from your beloved, the old Duke?" A hint of sarcasm lurked in her voice. I struggled to keep my temper.

"He was away in Spain when my sire died…and no, it was not worth raising forces and spilling blood for such a small, relatively worthless castle. One must choose their battles wisely. As it stands, my uncle threw me a few crumbs, no doubt in fear I might just seek my rightful inheritance, and I was content with that. What lands I possess are rather mean and I have seldom visited them, leaving stewards and bailiffs to run them on my behalf."

"Maybe it is time those living there saw their absent mistress." Aenor sipped on her own sherbet. Hers was flavoured with limes and coloured green like poison. It matched the tone of her voice, bitter and even faintly venomous. She had never truly forgiven me for leaving her as a child and I was a fool to think she was beginning to forget them.

I made to rise; I felt suddenly old, a pain in my back, a stiffness in my knees. "I think you may be right, daughter. I must spend the rest of my days far from here."

At that moment, little Eleanor ran over, eyes wide. She had heard all, despite pretending to be engrossed in her games with Petronilla. I had no doubt she would find such an art—listening with one ear— highly useful as she grew older. "Grandmama, do not leave us! You sing and tell stories better than *maman*! And let us stay up later, and eat more sweetmeats!"

Aenor rolled her eyes, but suddenly softened a little. "Your grandmama cannot stay here forever, Eleanor…just as one day you will have to leave. But…perhaps, not yet…" She glanced at me.

A little flame of hope kindled in my heart. I did not want to be packed away to my paltry lands, like some aged dowager. Even though my heart hurt every time I looked at a place in the palace where William and I had walked together, it was still *his* domain, imbued with his spirit. I felt close to him in Poitier. He was buried nearby with his ancestors in the abbey of Saint John the Evangelist at Montierneuf and I could visit his grave.

"At some point, when my little Aigret has grown a bit older and stronger, Will desires to make a pilgrimage to Saint James de Compostela." Aenor's eyes shone; I had no idea my daughter was pious enough to go on such a journey. "We have decided to take the children…You could accompany us and assist me."

"Is such travel wise?" I asked. It was a long hot journey to Spain and not even pilgrims on the road were all honest, decent men. There could be looters and brigands along the route, as well as the ever-present spectre of sickness.

"Their father will ride alongside us, with his men." She looked cross to hear my doubts. "It is up to you, mother. I should have thought you would wish this reprieve. To spend time with your grandchildren, before you must…"

"I will come," I said quickly.

It took some time for Will and Aenor to ready for their pilgrimage. Months passed and gradually the ache and tug of loss in my heart began to lessen just a little. Life had returned to the palace, with troubadours, musicians and poets once more in the hall and in the gardens. 'Little Willy' had changed with manhood and had begun to appreciate the finer arts, although his interests were far less earthy than his father's. The singers did not regale us with songs of bawdiness or hidden lusts; instead, there were songs of high deeds or religious chants to praise Mother Mary and her Son. While William had been known as The Troubadour, men had begun to call Will 'the Saint.' I still saw little in him I would call saintly, he was often petulant, hard-headed and moody, but men will see what they want to see...

At last, we rode away out of Poitou with cheering crowds waving us on. Will and Aenor rode astride on fine horses, waving to the masses and enjoying the pomp and adulation. I was in a chariot with Eleanor, Petronilla and William Aigret. The boy was now three, and curious, trying to rip the hangings open so that he could peek outside. I had brought supplies of violet-scented sugar from Damascus, funnel cake and *pipefarces*-cheese slices fried and breaded to distract him and keep him quiet. The girls and I indulged in them ourselves, of course, and before long we were all sated and sleepy, our bellies hurting from too much consumption.

It took as nigh on a week to reach our first major stop at Talmont, where we would rest a day or two before faring onwards. The church there was the first stop for pilgrims on the long trail to the Shrine of St James. I was glad in heart as we drew close; I could smell the scent of the waves of the Gironde Estuary, a cool sweet tang that spoke to me of freedom and adventure.

Talmont was a small village on an islet reached by a bridge; when the tides were very high, sometimes it was completely cut off from the mainland. The grey waves of the estuary roiled beyond it, and on the other side loomed the dark, pine-clad shores of Point de Grave.

The houses on the islet were neat and well-kept but it was not a big place; our destination was the huge Roman-styled church of St Radegonde that stood on the height of the promontory, overlooking the restless waters. The church dominated sea, sky and land, and white-winged birds wheeled above its peaked roof, shrieking and diving. A small chapel had stood there centuries ago, which had been replaced by Benedictines from the local Abbey of Saint John d'Angély to aid supplicants on their way to Spain where they would pray before the next leg of the journey across those moving waters.

Many pilgrim hostels clustered around the foot of St Radegonde's, and we disembarked at the largest and richest guest-house, run by the brothers of the Abbey. As members of our entourage scrambled to find haylofts or barns to sleep in, my daughter and I entered a stout stone building and waited in a neat but unexciting chamber for our valuables to be unloaded and brought in for safekeeping. We were all to share; the children and their nurses were in a small sub-chamber beside us, and the maids who served my daughter and me would sleep on straw pallets in the hall outside.

I moved the horn cover back off the slit window and stared out over the estuary, its sands and its mud glimmering dully. Several ships were moored at the cliff foot, waiting for us to board them on the morrow. "Look, Aenor," I said. "The ships! Is this not exciting?"

My daughter made no answer. I turned to look at her. She was slumped upon the simple bed, her face white and covered with a sheen of sweat.

"Aenor, what is the matter?" Immediately I dived to her side.

"It is nothing," she murmured, but her words were slurred. "Just the long ride in the sun. Or bad food at one of those wayside taverns."

I leaned over and touched her forehead. Her skin burnt like fire. I snatched my hand away, shocked. "This is not merely from the sun. I am going to find help."

Aenor began to complain, insisting she merely needed rest, but I ignored her protests and left the room, ordering her two women, who were dicing in the hall, to go and attend their mistress. I could not find Will but managed to locate the porter, a monk from the nearby abbey. "Is there a physic in the village or the monastery? The Lady Aenor is sick."

The man looked startled and was not terribly helpful. "A-are you sure it is necessary? Brother Infirmarer at the abbey is known for his healing arts, but it is a long way for him to travel if it is only for some woman's complaint…"

"How dare you!" Fists bunched, I stepped towards him; he was a short man and I towered over him like an Amazon. "You speak so lightly of the Duchess of Aquitaine? Go now, and fetch this Brother Infirmarer…or I will see you flogged, man of God or not!"

The monk made a fearful, high-pitched noise in his throat and stumbled for the open door of the guest house. He began to trudge away across the sandy headland. "Not on foot, your imbecile!" I shouted after him. "Get a horse from the damn stable! Or do I have to go myself and drag your healer back by his tonsure!"

Flushing beet-red, the monk darted for the stable, hoisting up his robes over his sandalled feet. I stood and watched, with hammering heart, as he galloped away from Talmont, flopping like an overstuffed sack over the horse's back.

"It is an ague; the one the Italians called Mal Aria, the Bad Air," said Brother Infirmarer after he had ridden from the abbey to the guest quarters at St Radegonde's and examined Aenor.

I stood with a fretting William in the far side of Aenor's sick chamber while her ladies came and went with bowls of water and buckets of vomit and excreta. Aenor had deteriorated even in the few hours it had taken for the monk to arrive; her skin had gone yellow, but more frightening, the whites of her eyes had also assumed that sickly hue. Despite the warmth of the room, she trembled as if it was winter, but still the sweat poured from her in streams.

"My head…it feels like it will burst!" she cried at one point, pressing her hands to her skull, and then she rolled over, curled in a tight ball, crying out that now it felt as if a hand was twisting her bowels and trying to rip them asunder.

"Do something!" I commanded Brother Infirmarer in desperation. "She will recover, with care, won't she?"

The monk blinked nervously and twisted his hands. "It is in God's hands, Lady. If you wish, I can bleed her…."

"Bleed her! You will not! She is weak enough!" William roared.

Brother Infirmarer began to stammer. "S-some say trepanning the skull can aid a patient suffering from *Mal Aria*…but I truly have not the skill needed for work so perilous."

"So, you say her recovery is purely in God's hands," I cried. "That there is nothing you can do."

"I fear so, Lady. Every year it happens thus, especially in places where there are marshes and bad air."

We had passed a few such boggy areas on our journey hither. I grabbed the arm of Brother Infirmarer's cassock and dragged him into the corridor outside, kicking the door shut so that Will and Aenor could not hear. "What are her chances of survival? Tell me the truth; I do not want false hope."

"Severe cases of *Mal Aria* almost always die, Madame," he said bluntly. "Although her Ladyship is at least lucid, which is a good sign, the extreme yellowness of face and eyes is worrisome. Adults do have a better chance of survival than young children, though…"

The children! My thoughts flew to my grandchildren, locked up with their nurses, who were trying to amuse them while we dealt with Aenor's illness.

Nausea clawed my gut. Even though Aenor had ridden alongside William while I rode with Eleanor, Petronilla and William Aigret in the chariot, we had still eaten the same food, stopped at the same inns, breathed the same tainted air….

"Brother Infirmarer, we have the young heir of Aquitaine and his sisters travelling with us. Is…is there any chance they might be…" The words died in my throat, strangled on my tongue, as the door of the children's bedchamber burst open and a nursemaid rushed out, colour high, tears streaming down her cheeks.

She saw me and tumbled at my feet, clawing at my knees with shaking hands. "Oh, Lady…oh Lady Dangereuse, help us, please! It is the baby! He is sick…Oh God, he is sick like Lady Aenor!"

The rest of the pilgrimage was cancelled. Instead of proceeding to Spain, our entourage trudged back to Poitiers, carrying two coffins, one painfully, tragically small, on the back of a pennant-laden funeral hearse. A few of our attendants—a nursemaid and a groom—had also succumbed to the ague called *Mal Aria*, but there was no money to bring them back to Poitiers and they were buried hastily in the graveyard of St Radegonde's next to the restless sea.

I sat in silent shock in my chariot with Eleanor and Petronilla weeping and red-eyed beside me. As we neared Poitier Palace, Eleanor grasped my sleeve and gazed at me with big, imploring eyes—'With Mama…gone to God, will you stay with us for good, grandmama?"

I placed my hand on her head with is thick, waving hair. "I do not know, child." I endeavoured to be honest. "That will be up to your father, the Duke."

Her small, pert face brightened. "I am sure he would be delighted to have you care for me and Petronilla."

I smiled back, but weakly; I was not as certain as my forward little granddaughter.

When Will summoned me to his audience chamber in the week after Aenor and William Aigret were interred near my dear heart William in the Abbey of Saint John the Evangelist, I was filled with a sense of foreboding. His face, as he sat high upon the dais, was etched with care, his mouth unsmiling and downturned. I had worn my most dour garb, to show that I was contrite and humble in presence—and also to remind him that I was mourning my daughter. He had lost a wife, but he could take another—I would never get my daughter back.

"Well, Lady," he said, "what is it you choose to do?"

"Choose? I have little choices, my lord Duke; I await *your* decision."

He looked down his nose at me; I remembered well the dislike he had borne me in the past. "Hm, a humbler Dangereuse? I am not sure whether to be pleased or wary."

"If you permit me to stay in Poitiers, I will oversee the girls' education," I said. "I promise you that they will be the best-educated maidens in Aquitaine—indeed, in all of Europe. They will be fit brides for...the highest of nobles, even for princes and kings."

He scratched his chin. "You are an intelligent woman, Dangereuse; I know this, for it was a quality my father admired, alongside great beauty. However, I am a little concerned. Although I do not object to my daughters being taught by you, I do not want either of them to *become* like you. Do you understand what I am saying?"

I nodded fervently. "Of course. They shall grow up obedient, pliant ...and chaste. My own...*mistakes* will not be repeated."

"Good." He nodded. "But be sure, I will keep a watch on my daughters' wellbeing, and if I am not happy with either their or your behaviour—I will bid you depart for your own lands at once. And if I decide that you are to leave Poitiers at any time, there will be no reprieve...you will not come here again."

So I took on the rearing of poor, lost Aenor's children and retained my abode in the fastness of the Maubergeon. I taught the girls of the work of Troubadours, like their grandsire—editing his bawdier compositions to make them acceptable for their tender ears. I had an old, white-bearded scholar come to tutor them in mathematics and sciences, just as if they were boys. They even learned the names and positions of the constellations, and I would point them out from the battlements—The Hunter with his bright Belt; Andromeda, daughter of Queen Cassiopeia, bound to a rock to be eaten by a sea monster, Charles's Wain that is also known as the Great Bear; hideous Hydra of the Many Heads, and dozens more. I also personally taught them the history of Aquitaine and Poitou, recited their own noble genealogy until they knew their ancestors' names back to front, and found books for them to study on important places in the world—Rome, Greece, Spain, Paris, the Holy Land. Naturally, I also taught the things considered necessary for young noblewomen—stitchery, weaving and spinning, and an ability to keep accounts and run a tidy household. Latin lessons were also imperative, although both girls despised them and whined when told to bring out their books—I tempted them to obedience by saying that if they were very good in their lessons, we would go riding or hawking afterwards. Both were tall active girls who loved galloping around on horseback and participating in the excitement of a hunt, and they were unusually strong in both body and mind. I supposed some of that had come from me, and occasionally my granddaughters were headstrong or impertinent and there would be a battle of wills, especially with Eleanor.

But I always won in the end.

I thought that Will might wed again, but it seemed with Aenor's death he had lost his taste for women altogether, not that he ever had his father's carnal appetites. He did once announce himself betrothed to one Emma of Limousin, the heiress to Limoges, but his enemy, the Count of Angouleme, abducted her one night and married her himself. Aquitaine held its collective breath, wondering if he might go to war over Emma...but he shrugged off the grave insult from Angouleme; his heart had not been in the union anyway.

What he had *not* lost his taste for rich food, though—indeed, it had increased dramatically. Banquets were held with growing frequency and delicious delights heaped on trenchers for the guests. William grew increasingly stout until he almost resembled a barrel wrapped in furs. He puffed when he walked and his visage was red as fire when he ascended the Palace's many staircases. It was not a healthy state for any man, and I am certain his father would have been outraged at his son's growing sloth and greed, but I was in no position to challenge his ways.

The girls did not appear to notice his girth, though. It was papa this, papa that. They seemed to regard him as some jolly figure of fun, a giant, lumbering bear who would roar and gather them, shrieking with delighted laughter, into his embrace.

But he was frequently not so jolly in private, not when it came to managing his domains. He fought with the Lusignans, an ever fractious and grasping family, and with the Larchevêque clan of Parthenay, who had proven troublesome for years. Their name meant 'The Archbishops' and they truly thought God was on their side in every matter imaginable. Lord Ebbo Larchevêque had once fought a duel with my William beneath the walls of his impregnable castle, even though William was, by all rights, his liege lord. Now Ebbo's boorish and violent sons were showing signs of being equally as obnoxious as their father.

When not dealing with local affray, Will also embroiled himself in affairs in Normandy, aiding Geoffrey of Anjou to take the Duchy by right of his wife. I was quite curious to see this Geoffrey, who was named 'le Bel' for his handsome looks and who wore a golden sprig of broom in his stylish hat but, alas, he never came to Poitiers. News reached us that Geoffrey had been wounded in the foot and the Norman campaign was at an end.

I wondered what should happen if Will were to die in battle…Well, Eleanor would be Duchess of Aquitaine, and that I was sure would bring a host of suitors both fair and foul to seek her hand…and the wealth it brought. And I would be her sole protector, the disgraced, adulteress grandmother. The thought made me grind my teeth in fear at the thought.

I tried to keep my fears close, so as not to disrupt Eleanor and Petronilla's schooling, but it was difficult to keep them from occasionally showing. I attempted to calm myself by engaging in many activities, including the final preparations for my daughter Sybille to join the order of the Benedictine nuns at Saintes. Henri had already gone to Cluny to become a monk the previous year. Henri had always been of monkish temperament, but Sybille was less placid and religious, and I felt a pang of guilt that I had determined her fate so young, but she knew her duty and accepted it without complaint. In that way, she resembled neither me nor her father…

The Duke returned from his failed incursion into Normandy having seen little battle. The girls screamed with happiness and hurled themselves at him, before their nurses, seeing my stern look, pulled them away and reminded them to behave like proper young damsels.

William had lost some of his bulk while on campaign, but dark bags hung beneath his eyes and his hair hung lank about his shoulders. "I am weary," he said to me after he had dined and bathed. I strolled alongside him in the garden, watching as the girls—really young women now—cavorted between the trimmed hedges and flower beds in some childish game of hide-and-seek. "I feel I might need some solace on my knees before our Lord. I want to take a journey to the shrine of St James. It was such a bitter blow the other time, when…when…" He dropped his head and crossed himself.

I crossed myself too. "It is in the past. Aenor and William Aigret lie safe in God's keeping. You may not have a male heir, but you should be proud of Eleanor. She is an exceptional child. William, now that you have returned, you should think of a marriage for her, to preserve all she will inherit if you do not remarry yourself. You know what might happen otherwise…"

He nodded, a bitter smile on his sun-roughened lips. "The wolves would come out to play. Yes, you are right, Dangereuse. I have been thinking…"

"You have someone in mind."

"Yes, but I dare not speak of it yet—not to you, not to Eleanor. It may all come to nothing." He leaned forward on his seat, hands splayed on his knees. "Be that as it may— any marriage is some time in the future. For now, I want my daughters to accompany me as far as Bordeaux from whence I will fare to the Shrine of St James in Spain. If you wish, you may accompany them. Pray God, this time my journey will be successful, without the desperate sorrow of the last."

A chill ran down my spine despite the warmth of the day. It was as if by his words, his veiled reference to the deaths of Aenor and William Aigret, he had doomed this new enterprise…but that was superstitious tomfoolery. Only God could decide such things.

"I will happily accompany you, Eleanor and Petronilla to Bordeaux, and act as chaperone to the girls," I said, bowing my head.

CHAPTER THIRTEEN

We set out for Santiago de Compostela following the same course we took nigh on seven years ago. The church of St Radegonde rose up, overlooking its cliff and the waters beyond. This time, no illness afflicted any of the party, and we crossed on the waiting vessels, my granddaughters clinging to the ship's rails, laughing and screaming in mock fear as the gulls dived through the riggings and the ship rolled on the gentle waves. Reaching the far side, we proceeded on to the teeming city of Bordeaux where we were given hospitality by Archbishop Geoffrey de Lauroux in the Ombriere Palace, a mighty fortress built into a corner of the Roman wall that surrounded the ancient towns. The girls acted with delight, letting misty spray from the palace's tall fountains blow upon their hot faces and wandering under strange, exotic trees that thrived in the warmer climes.

However, as their father prepared to depart, changing his garments for the sackcloth of a humble penitent and pinning a cockleshell pilgrim's badge to his shoulder, they began to fret and complain, particularly Eleanor. She knelt before her father, tears in her eyes, batting those long lashes I knew would one day entrance most men who gazed upon them. "Sire, I beg a boon, for me and for Petronilla. Please do not leave us here!"

"I thought you liked it in Ombriere—you certainly seemed to when we arrived and you ran about the place like a whirlwind," said Will. "Has the archbishop not shown you kindness and hospitality?"

"Yes, he has, father…but we would still go with you. In fact, Archbishop Lauroux even said he would not be averse to going along himself! Spain is so far…and in your pilgrim's garb you look so sad and alone!"

He gave a doleful little laugh. "It is a long journey and the route may be perilous."

"Petronilla and I are not afraid. Grandmama could come with us too, and she is afraid of nothing!"

He glanced over at me, standing with my head bowed behind my outspoken granddaughter and her sister. "Madame? What say you?"

I took a deep breath. "It would enhance their education…and to join upon such a noble pilgrimage is never an idle pursuit."

He inclined his head. "Make ready then, as quickly as possible. Tell the Archbishop he may accompany me if it is his wish. We will all travel together to Santiago de Compostela."

Onwards we went, Archbishop Lauroux with us. William walked afoot in his pilgrim grey, while we rode in a plain unmarked chariot guarded by a handful of his knights, and the Archbishop and his attendants rode along behind. Over the awe-inspiring Pyrenees we fared, where craggy peaks prodded an azure sky and fat cows munched the verdant grass in vast upland pastures filled with vivid wildflowers. Between marvelling at the mountains, Eleanor read Petronilla and me sections from Will's book, the *Codex Calixtinus*, a guide for pilgrims. Some of it was quite scandalous, eliciting giggles from the girls. I had to frown at them but inwardly I was amused too.

"The book says Basques and Navarrese would kill a Frenchman for a pittance!" exclaimed Eleanor.

"Oh, don't tell me that!" Petronilla covered her ears. "I don't want to be scared by every sound I hear tonight!"

"That's not all. The Basques wear horns round their neck and carry spears. They can howl like a wolf or whistle like a bird, which serves as a secret kind of language when they prepare an ambush. It is thought they descend from Scots brought here by Caesar."

"What's a 'Scot'?" asked Petronilla, perplexed.

Eleanor frowned. "I am not really sure, but I gather some kind of northern barbarian..." She continued on and suddenly reddened to the tips of her ears. "God help us, the guide says these wild tribes have...have *congress* with their beasts of burden, and that they like to kiss a woman's c..."

"That's enough, Eleanor." I reached out and took the book from her. "This book is meant for the leader of the party, your father...not for the eyes of a young innocent maid."

"Not so innocent now, after reading that," smirked Petronilla.

"Hush," I said. I put the book behind me so they could not get it. I would read it myself later when they went to sleep.

Eventually our party reached the mountainous Pass of Cize, the gateway into Spain. The mountain was so high it seemed as if we were almost touching heaven. Huge birds of prey swept overhead, harsh cries echoing throughout the wilderness. On the top, we took in the view—the glimmering seas of Brittany with the cold Atlantic beyond, and the green and brown lands of Aragon, Castille and France. All around us stood rows of crosses, some tall and ornate, others humble and wind-bitten, fading into the coarse spring tufts of grass.

"Were there dead men buried here?" I asked Will uneasily. The wind pulled at my veil, seeking to rip it from my head.

"No," he said. "This place is known as Charlemagne's Cross. He stopped here once when entering Spain and raised a cross. Others, on their own quests now do likewise."

We descended from that dizzying height, passing a church and hostel a mighty cleft rock that was said to have been split by the sword blows of the hero Roland. We then made for Roncesvalles, where Roland had perished in a ferocious battle with the infidel, and where we spent the night.

Then we were on deep into Spain, halting at the sacred places of pilgrimage at Pamplona, Lograno, Burgos. As our entourage reached Leon, Eleanor was chattering to Petronilla, who was finding the heat unbearable and lay with our solitary maid fanning her and sprinkling rosewater on her brow.

"Oh, Petra, do cheer yourself! This is terribly exciting and you are missing it all!" Eleanor leaned over her sister and prodded her with a finger.

"My head hurts," complained Petronilla. "If I stick my head outside, I am sure the sun will burn me dark as a peasant girl."

Eleanor had been walking beside her father for a little while; although she had worn a heavy headdress the sun had indeed given her face a light golden sheen. "I must get asses' milk to rub on my face like Cleopatra!" she said knowledgeably.

"We're not in Egypt," said Petronella with scorn.

"But there must be asses…somewhere around," said Eleanor. "The Romans were here once, you know, just as they were in Egypt. They called the road we travel upon 'the route of the Milky Way'. Think of it, Petra—a wondrous trail of stars!"

"I call it dull…and hot. And the stars are not out now, only a blazing sun." Petronilla rolled over and grabbed an orange from a nearby basket. Peeling it, she bit into it and sighed blissfully. "At least the oranges are nice here…so fresh and never shrivelled inside."

Eleanor was crawling over to the window of the chariot, despite the chastisement of our tired-looking maid. "You do not want all those foreigners gawping at you, my Lady. I heard what they get up to…in that…that nasty book you read from."

Eleanor ignored her and stuck her head out. I smiled to myself. I could see myself in both girls, but the eldest in particular. She must learn to contain herself though if her father planned the high marriage he had suggested. I let her look a little longer at the thick town walls of Leon with their Roman bases and the hundreds of spires and towers beyond, and then motioned her back inside. She hesitated, saw my stern look, and obeyed with a sigh.

"We shall stay here tonight; your father will visit the shrines of St Isidore and St Pelagius, the boy-saint martyred by the Moors," I said, "then we will begin the final leg of the pilgrimage to the tomb of St James."

"I cannot wait," said Eleanor. She was wearing a scallop shell pilgrim badge in silver with a cross graven upon it. "How long has it taken? Nearly a month I reckon!"

I nodded. "Yes, your reckoning is correct. It is a long journey. It is the first time for me also. I am so glad your father permitted me to travel with you."

"He *likes* you much better now," she said, with all the tactless honesty of youth. "I am glad he let you continue to live Poitiers as our governess."

"I am glad, too, Eleanor," I said softly, although with a trace of sadness. She would marry soon, and Petronilla probably not long after her sister…and where would I be then? But I said nothing of my fears; I would not spoil her excitement for the pilgrimage.

"On the final leg of the road to St James's shrine, we will travel before first light to avoid the worst of the heat," I told her. "Your father told me he is feeling the warmth as much as Petra. We can both look out the chariot then, with no fear of being leered at by strangers. Together, Eleanor, we shall look up at that Milky Way the Romans saw. Together, we will watch the procession of the summer stars!"

Santiago de Compostela was heaving with pilgrims. Dawn had come and gone and although it was still early the streets were packed with all manner of humanity, from great lords wearing incongruous sackcloth yet with silk canopies billowing overhead to the poorest of the poor— those blind, maimed, scarred, clad in rags and hobbling on crutches. Even though noon was long away, the heat already made shimmering waves over town and wall. Dust rose in clouds beneath the feet of horses, mules and people. Bells tolled and the strident cries of hawkers filled the air. Traders held up handfuls of scallop shell pilgrim badges. Bakers placed their wares on ledges to waft tempting smells across the streets. Livestock grunted and surged, beaten into wooden corrals by their masters.

Duke William was sick. He had shown signs of being unwell in Burgos but had waved his physician away when the man counselled that he should rest. "It is only the heat!" William had snapped, his cheeks mottled and his hands shaking. "God's Teeth, a headache won't stop me from completely my pilgrimage. My father was a Crusader; it was a bloody sight hotter where he travelled. Yet you expect me to lie abed like some weak woman? Away with you, man!"

Now, in Santiago de Compostela, the extent of his illness was evident. He had fallen from his horse as we rode in during the night, barely conscious, his mouth slack and drooling. Eleanor, gazing out from our chariot only minutes before he fell, had seen a shooting star arc over the dome of heaven and burn out at the edge of the firmament.

Now she was weeping bitterly, inconsolably, for she believed the star was an omen that her father would die.

Mayhap she was right.

Santiago was full of abbeys, priories, hostelries and hospitals. Our company sought refuge in an abbey, and William was carried, groaning, on a bier into the infirmary, his own physician and Archbishop Lauroux at his side. The monks looked solemn; when the abbot came to bring news, it was not good. Their Brother Infirmarer said it was poisoning from ingesting rotten food or tainted water, and he had become very weak and was passing blood. He also had gone without drinking for too long, which made the condition even more perilous.

"What will happen if he dies out here?" Petronilla said in a small, weak voice. "What will become of us in a strange land?"

"Nothing," I said firmly. "No harm will come to you. He will not die…and if it is God's will he does, all the men of the entourage will now be loyal to Eleanor."

But Eleanor was a female, not a warrior for all her spirit, and I knew well what could happen…

Later in the day, I went out to pray at the saint's shrine. I took Eleanor and Petronilla, heavily veiled against the heat and prying eyes, along with an unobtrusive guard or two. The cathedral of St James was a work in progress, having once been burnt down by the Moors. Although the basic structure had been completed some fifteen years ago, new stonework and embellishments were being added all the time, expanding the size of the building to impressive proportions.

My granddaughters and I entered the precinct through a sea of granite and marble pillars, watched over by statues of the saints and prophets and leered at by rows of carved grotesques. Above the door, a vast tympanum showed a scene of demons assailing Christ; on the left, a throned King David played the rebec, while on the right a half-clad woman lounged upon a lion, whilst holding a skull in her hands. Eve? Or some Biblical adulteress reaping the wages of her sin?

I eyed the carving solemnly—was this a warning for me, who had been that adulteress, wild-haired and flaunting her body joyously, not so long ago? I had left that life behind now, though—there would never be another man to share my bed. But that was as close to repentance as I would ever come.

The cathedral's darkness embraced me and the girls, warm and smelling of incense and tallow—and, less fragrantly, of the bodies of supplicants, long unwashed. Pilgrims of all statures in life filed towards the altar where the Saint's bones lay in a silver casket laden with offerings and surrounded by candles. Monks were keeping the faithful in line, making sure they did not overwhelm those already there before them, the frail cripples, the staggering blind, the maimed who begged for the return of their former health.

We had nearly reached the shrine when a disturbance broke out in the masses of people queued behind us. I could hear a male voice shouting, its tone filled with urgency. An uneasy murmur went through the throng and heads craned around. The monks looked peeved at such a noise breaking the silence of this sanctified place. The next moment, a young man thrust his way forcefully through the crowd and approached the altar, his shoes sliding and slipping on the tiles in the greatness of his speed.

I recognised him at once; one of Duke Will's body-servants, a lad called Piers. I heard a small gasp from Eleanor; felt her stiffen at my side. Petronilla reached for her sister's hand, her face whitening.

Panting, the youth glanced around, looking, seeking. Sweat soaked his hair, gathered on his lip.

"Piers!" I called in a low whisper, moving past an old blind woman with a stick. "We are here."

Piers stumbled towards us. He ignored me but bowed before Eleanor and Petronilla. "My Lady Eleanor, thank God I have found you. You must come at once. The Duke calls for you. The physician says it is urgent, that he will not…will not…" He shook his head, stricken dumb by grief

"Come, grandchildren," I ordered, beckoning to the tearful girls. "We must do as we are asked and return to your father at once."

With Piers in the lead, we fled the cathedral, leaving pilgrims, priests, monks and nuns staring after us in astonishment. Soon we reached the abbey where we lodged and were escorted by a grave-faced Brother to the chamber where the Duke lay ill.

At the door, Brother Infirmarer put out a hand to stop us. "I regret to say his condition has worsened. I fear he has had some kind of apoplectic fit…a stroke of God…even though the symptoms are not the usual ones. Sometimes men can survive such events if the fit is mild, but they are seldom as they were. His other complaints add additional problems. He is declining rapidly and I fear…"

"And what do *you* say?" I snapped at Will's personal physician, who hovered near the bedside, head bowed.

"Sadly, I must agree with the good Brother," he said. "I fear…he will not recover."

"Let me go to him!" cried Eleanor, pulling away from me and thrusting herself past the monk blocking her way.

She flung herself down at her father's bedside, clutching his hand, which lay limp and sweaty in her own. Petronilla followed after, running to Eleanor's side.

"Thank you for your candour," I said to the Infirmarer, "and for preparing us for the worst," and then I too moved past him and, heavy with trepidation, entered the infirmary chamber.

Lying on a mean pallet, William, son of my William, looked an aged man; it was as if a wizard had cast a deadly spell over him, giving him an extra forty years. His cheeks were sunken and one eyelid drooped unnaturally. His entire visage was rigid and ashen, the muscles frozen into a contorted grimace. Petronilla took one look, cried out, and turned away, weeping.

I crossed myself. His condition was indeed grave; that was clear even to my untrained eye.

"Come closer, Eleanor," Will grated, his voice dry and rasping. Drool ran from the corner of his mouth. She leaned over him, despairing, tears glistening on her lashes. "I am soon to go to God, daughter, but first I must speak to you …"

"You will *live!*" she cried, shaking her head. Her veil fell off; dark hair touched by hints of fire tumbled down in heavy waves. "I command that you live!"

He tried to smile but failed, for the muscles that moved his mouth no longer worked correctly. "None can command Death, daughter—not even one so fair as you. Now, listen to me, while you were gone, I made final provisions for you after my death. I had not told you before, believing there was so much time still to be had…but I have been negotiating with Louis, the French King these past months. He is set to be your guardian when I die…"

"The French King, Louis the Fat? But he is old and sickly and…"

"He is a *King*, Eleanor, those things are of no matter…but there is more you must know. I told him of your beauty, your talents, your outstanding learning…and he wishes for his son and heir, Louis the Younger, to marry you. You will one day be Queen of France as well as Duchess of Aquitaine. With a Prince as a husband, your rights to the duchy will be well-protected."

"What about me?" cried Petronilla, panicked, obviously fearing she would be separated from her sister.

"I—I have not had time to make a good match for you, my little Pet. But you shall go to court with Eleanor as a companion and no doubt a fitting husband will be found for you in time…" He made a wheezing noise and clutched his chest. His gaze, strained and tortured, travelled to the Brother Infirmarer. "The Archbishop…I beg you call for my friend Archbishop Lauroux…to give the rites of Extreme Unction. I fear it is time; my eyes…I can no longer see well. I feel as if I am falling into a dark pit…Let me make my peace with God…"

The monk rushed out of the room, and I stepped away from the bed and ascended the three worn steps leading out of the chamber, giving my granddaughters a few moments of privacy with their dying father. Outside, I sat gasping warm air in the cloister, watching the rustling leaves of the vines that twined round its graceful pillars and arches.

William X had made provisions for his daughters after his demise…but there was nothing for me, his mother's one-time rival, nor had I expected there to be.

I was lost.

William was buried before the high altar of the cathedral of St James the Great, near the shrine he had not lived to see. It was a fitting place under the swinging silver censer that billowed out sweet incense fragrance. Not much time could be spent in mourning, however. William had appointed Archbishop Geoffrey as the girls' temporary guardian until Prince Louis could claim his bride and take her to his sire's court in Paris. The archbishop was eager to return to Bordeaux, and so hurried us on the road. Perhaps this was a good thing—for when we arrived at his palace, a message was waiting from King, who was at a hunting lodge recovering from one of the many ailments caused by his girth and age. The King informed Geoffrey that he was sending his son Louis to Bordeaux forthwith and there he would marry Eleanor without delay. Clearly, the French royals were eager to have Aquitaine in their possession, even if only by marriage.

My granddaughters were subdued as we awaited the arrival of the prince. I tried to cheer them with little stories and tales but their smiles were few.

"I wonder what Louis will be like," mused Eleanor. "I hope he is not gross like his sire."

"You've never seen King Louis. You cannot say he is 'gross,'" I chided.

"*Everyone* says it." Disdainful, she tossed her head. "He is so gross he cannot see his jewelled shoes when he walks."

"He is a king and his son is a king-to-be. 'Grossness' can be overlooked in kings. Don't you wish to be a queen?"

"Yes, but..." Her lip quivered. "I...I also want someone I...I can love, someone to desire, just like in the Troubadours' Songs."

"Oh, Eleanor, they are just songs."

"But it was not that way for you, was it? You left my grandsire Aimery to abide with my grandsire William in the Maubergeon Tower."

I sighed, suddenly weary. "Yes...yes, it is true, but I am hardly a shining example of a good woman. I am not who you should aspire to be."

She fell silent and looked thoughtful at that.

I gnawed a nail in frustration and worry. Eleanor was, in truth, very like me in her headstrong ways, but by God's Blood, I did not want her to tread the same path. Too dangerous. In the case of a royal bride, too treasonous.

Nigh on three months later, Eleanor wed Prince Louis in the cathedral of St Andrew in Bordeaux. He had arrived with a great party of French nobles and bishops several weeks before.

I viewed him from afar and was glad to see he was not as 'gross' as his ailing father. In fact, he was slender as a reed, even on the scrawny side, with a pale complexion, high forehead and long fair hair like silk. He spoke and moved quietly, without the braggadocio of many young men, most likely because he had been earmarked for the monastery when his elder brother, Philip, was alive. He was very friendly with the churchmen of his entourage, seeming more at ease with them than lords or soldiers, especially the powerful Abbot Suger who had tutored him at the monastery of St Denis. Suger was even at his side now, dogging his every step, watching his every move, preaching at him about how a Christian prince should behave.

"I was not always meant to be King," he told Eleanor on their first meeting in the garden of Archbishop Geoffrey's palace. Suger was lurking by the fountain, his expression one of fusty disapproval as if he feared his charge and his betrothed might leap at each other and engage in unbridled sin before all onlookers. I receive the impression Suger would have preferred some timid slip of a thing as a wife for his protégé; a girl too in awe of a royal prince to do more in his presence than squeak like a mouse and blush.

"Oh, what happened?" asked Eleanor, ever curious. I noticed Suger's thin lips purse in irritation.

"I had an older brother who was father's heir…but he died. It was most tragic. Philip fell over a pig. Or rather, his horse did. He hit his head upon the cobblestones, fell down senseless and never woke again. I was so upset, Eleanor, not just because my brother was dead, but because. I loved the abbey. I wanted to be a monk, not a king."

She had looked bewildered then. "But you do now want to be king, I presume? And you are happy to be marrying me?"

"Ah…oh of course," Louis blundered, turning scarlet to the tips of his ears. "Our wedding shall be marvellous, dear Eleanor."

The ceremony certainly *was* marvellous. The members of the Capet dynasty loved multiple crownings. Louis had already been coronated once, at Reims, as a young boy— now he received his crown again, as a bridegroom, and Eleanor was crowned beside him, resplendent in a gown of blue silk and gold with ermine trim. Never had I seen a bride more beautiful, and my eyes moistened despite my best effort.

I prayed Louis would make her a fitting husband—and above all, forget his monkish reticence. I suspected Eleanor would want passion more than prayer, bed sheets before rosary beads.

Eleanor's nuptials, and the multitude of feasts and tourneys that accompanied them, had barely finished when a messenger came riding through the August heat, bedraggled and sweat-soaked from his long journey. He wore King Louis' colours and was ushered immediately into Prince Louis' presence. Courtiers saw the young prince pale, and Suger ushered him into a private room with the messenger in tow.

Within the next few hours, all men in Bordeaux knew that Louis the Fat had despaired of life at last. Shouts of *"Long Live the King!"* rang through the monastery where Louis and Eleanor were spending their first days of married life.

And long live the Queen, my granddaughter.

The newlywed couple travelled on to Poitiers where they were greeted by impressive crowds, all goggling at Eleanor and hurling flowers. They had seen her many times over the years, of course, but now she was a Queen as well as the Duchess of Aquitaine—she was transformed, as if by magic, to a mysterious creature raised on high by God's own will. I travelled with the company but was excluded in most things by the nobles of Fat Louis' court, whose loyalties had now passed to his son. There were even great ladies appointed to look after my granddaughters—as if I was not capable of doing so! Eleanor and Petronilla did try to find time to see me whenever it was possible, but invariably they were whisked away to perform other duties.

Another coronation was held at Poitiers Cathedral—the real, final one this time. The nave was packed and I, with many onlookers, stood outside. The great lords of France were inside with the new King and Queen and the bevvies of bishops and archbishops.

As the party left the cathedral and began heading toward the road that led to Paris, I glimpsed Eleanor once seated in a litter, Petronilla with her as a lady-in-waiting, and surrounded by a gaggle of haughty ladies of the court. She spied me in the crowd and I fancied a flash of sorrow darkened her face...then she was gone, lost amidst the crowds.

Somewhat heavy-hearted, I returned to Poitiers Palace and the Maubergeon. I noted that many of the castle's officers were different. The one I was familiar with had been replaced by servants of Louis. One tall, officious fellow with a nose like an eagle's beak lurched towards me as I walked towards the tower's entrance. "You are the Lady Dangereuse de l'Isle Bouchard?"

"I am," I said, rather icily. I could tell by his mannerisms he held a low opinion of me, even though we had only met that instant.

"His Grace the King has visited all the rooms in the Palace and has ordered that they be redecorated anew—including this Tower." He gestured dismissively to the Maubergeon as if it was an ugly thing, an eyesore in need of tearing down...not the font of my deepest and most cherished memories.

"And what did my granddaughter, the Queen, say?"

"Her Grace said nothing. It would not be her place to do so. She stands behind her husband and her King as is appropriate for every consort, and as God commanded."

So, my fears were coming true at last. I would have to leave Poitiers and retire to one of the tiny backwaters I had inherited. I wondered if 'Little Willy' had planned this when he had negotiated Eleanor's betrothal to Louis. One small, final act of revenge for his mother Philippa. Well, it mattered not...without my granddaughters here, there was no real reason why I should stay. All that was left were memories...memories and ghosts of the past.

"Will I have time to collect my goods?" I asked. "Or will you and your minions toss my belongings outside the gates in a heap?"

"Take as long as you need, my Lady," he said, face impassive.

"I will," I sniped, but I lied. I was now desperate to leave the palace. I would go home, to my childhood haunts, where I would retire in peace.

EPILOGUE

The garden is sweet, soft and misted after a brief rain shower. It is not vast and ornate like the gardens of the Palace of Poitiers, but I am content.

Contentment. It is a strange thing, but as the years have stretched on, I am a firebrand no more. The passion has burnt out and simple things—the herbs, the flowers, my little manor house with my handful of loyal servants are all I desire.

Sometimes I see my children from my marriage to Aimery; they have forgiven me my trespasses and there are more grandchildren to dandle or delight with wooden toys and poppets. On rare occasions, I journey to visit Henri or Sybille, both content in their religious vocations. I am glad of it. I have not seen Eleanor or Petronilla since the day Eleanor became a Queen; their lives are bound with the good and great...and also the not-so-good. Petra got herself involved with the King's cousin, Raoul, a one-eyed rogue many years her elder. I suppose she found his patch-eyed look dangerous and exciting. I might have done the same once. There was one catch in their entanglement, though—one I knew well. Raoul was already married. He put his wife, Eleonore of Champagne, aside to dwell with Petronilla, but failed to take into account the anger of her brother, Thibaud, a powerful and hot-headed warrior with a strong sense of pride. I had noticed him strutting about in Eleanor's wedding party; a louring, hulk of a man with bristling yellow hair. Thibaud roused the church against Raoul, and both Raoul and Louis found themselves excommunicated. All of this was so familiar to me. I was quite amused when his Holiness, Pope Innocent, called Louis, "A child in need of instruction.'

But not so familiar to me was the carnage that followed. Acting the fool to prove his manhood, Louis charged into Thibauld's lands and attacked the town of Vitry, where the King's soldiers torched the town—even the church where women and children huddled in fear, believing they were safe in God's House. Thousands of innocents died that day, and the horror of it reached far beyond France in black legend. Louis soon repented of his evil deed, and chided violently by Abbot Suger, became a penitent, humbling himself before the bones of St Denis and wearing a hair shirt beneath his robes.

His remorse seemed to pay off, for God soon granted him and Eleanor a child—not the longed-for son, alas, but a girl they named Marie for the Virgin. Shortly after, Louis' excommunication was lifted.

You would think that would be the end of it and the beginning of a happy and more peaceful reign—but no. There was a new Pope, Eugenius, and a new crusade, which Louis joined with holy fervour. He took Eleanor with him. Oh, how I enjoyed listening to tales of her adventures from travellers who sought meat and bread at my manor. My doors were always open to such. At Vezeley, I was informed, she had sat on a dais, dressed in the garb of a crusader, the cross stitched to the shoulder of her cloak. She had knelt before Bernard of Clairvaux to receive the Cross and later, witnessed Louis taking up the fire-red Oriflamme of France upon its golden lance. In Constantinople, that fair city of dream, she had dined in splendour with the Empress Eirene, before crossing the fabled Bosphorus on fleet Byzantine ships, rocking on the waves under blood-red sunsets and canopies of strange stars until they reached the lands of Asia.

And there…it all went wrong. The baggage train was attacked on Mount Cadmus to great loss, though the French army managed to soldier on to Antioch, with Eleanor riding in the van. It was in Antioch that whispers first surfaced that Louis was living like a monk, believing chastity to be the only appropriate state for a crusader, even a married one; he had not visited Eleanor's tent for months, nor had she sought his. And the ruler of Antioch was Eleanor's own uncle, Raymond, called by some the 'most handsome man on earth.' They struck up a close friendship…Well, I hope it was merely a friendship, for bedding one's uncle would be a step too far, even for someone as tolerant as me, but whatever the truth, unsavoury rumours began to fly.

At Raymond's court, Eleanor had told many courtiers, according to my sources, 'Louis and I are related within forbidden degrees. I am troubled and think we should no longer live as husband and wife.' None listened overmuch to her words, though, for let us speak the truth—who, in noble circles, is not related in one way or another? A close blood-tie is what papal dispensations are for…

Louis almost dragged her from Raymond's castle, her protestations known and sniggered at by all, and off they went on the next leg of his ill-fated Crusade. Damascus was their ultimate target, but God clearly had not smiled on their quest, for all they managed to capture were some apple trees in the orchards. At length, as starvation loomed on the horizon, the sorry crusaders made their way home, battling pirates and illness along the way—Eleanor fell ill upon the Isle of Sicily, and was bedridden for nigh on a month. Thank God, I did not know of her affliction till long after—I would have been frantic with worry. But she was strong, she recovered her strength and headed back towards France—despite the dreadful news that her beloved Uncle Raymond had been slain, his head embalmed and sent in a silver box as a gift for the Caliph of Baghdad.

Later that year, Eleanor bore another child to Louis, a girl they named Alice. At least occasionally the King does not act the part of a holy monk, it would seem, and I am sure, if he remembers *his* marital duties, Eleanor will eventually bear many strong, handsome boys. Sometimes these things take time.

But he is too busy to beget more children right now, of course. Trouble looms closer to home. He is at loggerheads with Henry of Normandy, a youth of seventeen, son of Maude, Empress of Germany, and Geoffrey of Anjou, that famously comely fellow who wore the sprig of golden broom and called himself *Plantagenet* after it. From all reports, young Henry is as strong as a bull and wily as a fox, and would surely have little pale Louis for his dinner if they fought one on one. But a peace treaty is going to be brokered soon, with Henry going to court to meet with Louis.

I wonder what Eleanor will make of him…

I ease myself back onto my garden seat, remove my shoes despite the impropriety of being barefoot in public, and feel the soil between my toes damp from the earlier rain-showers. My goblet is in my hand, rippling with wine the hue of life's blood. With it, I toast life, what I have left of it, for I am now gone seventy—a very great age—and muse upon the words my dearest William wrote so long ago…

"I enjoin my friends, upon my death,

to come hence to do me great honour,
since I have held both joy and delight
far and near, and in my own abode."

THE END

AUTHOR'S NOTES—

Dangereuse, the grandmother of Eleanor of Aquitaine, always intrigued me, not least because of her unusual name (also sometimes listed as Dangerosa). It wasn't her real name, which is unknown, although some historians think her birth-name may have been Amauberge. Very little is known about her but what little there is certainly intrigues—like her famous granddaughter, she lived her own life with little care about what others thought. Far from the idea that many people have about medieval women.

As in my novel, Dangereuse did indeed leave her husband Aimery of Châtellerault, having been abducted by his liege lord, William the Troubadour. It would seem the 'abduction' was not in the least distasteful to the lady, who lived with William until his death. She stayed with him at Poitiers in a Tower he built for her and bore him several children; she already had a number of children by her abandoned husband. The exact number of her offspring is unknown and some of those listed are almost certainly incorrect, so I randomly used the listed names of some but not others. For instance, 'Adelaide' is listed in one source as a daughter of Dangereuse and William, but the birth year given is years before her supposed parents met. Raymond/Ramon of Antioch is occasionally listed as being a son of Dangereuse and William, but almost certainly he is the son of William and his former wife, Philippa.

William's chequered marital history is likewise confusing. Frequently one runs across stories about his first wife being a lady called Ermengarde, who was rather unstable and troublesome. However, many historians now believe the solitary source for Ermengarde's existence is flawed, and that the chronicler confused her with another woman. Stories of a vengeful first wife who colluded with the second while both were in Fontevraud Abbey did exist, however, so William may indeed have had a troubled first wife, though maybe her name was not Ermengarde.

In my novel, I have William the Younger taking his daughters down to Santiago de Compostela on his fatal pilgrimage. They probably, in reality, remained in Bordeaux. However, one source says they were looked after while their father was away by the Archbishop Geoffrey de Lauroux and in another that the archbishop went to Spain with William, so I decided to have all of them go together.

All poems attributed to William the Troubadour are my versions of his actual work. He wrote some very bawdy stuff! It is also apparently true that he did paint a naked Dangereuse on the front of his shield.

The 'guidebook' Eleanor reads from on the journey to Santiago de Compostela is also a real book, most probably the first of its kind, telling pilgrims the routes to take and what they should visit on their journey. It also is full of warnings on everything from poisoned rivers to ferocious Basque and Navarrese warriors, who were given very unflattering descriptions!

There are no biographies solely on Dangereuse, for obvious reasons—she is just too obscure. Marion Meade's biography of Eleanor of Aquitaine does mention her, however, and gives a vivid description of the lands, towns and lifestyle she and her granddaughter would have known.

OTHER WORKS BY J.P. REEDMAN

RICHARD III and THE WARS OF THE ROSES:

I, RICHARD PLANTAGENET I: TANTE LE DESIREE. Richard in his own first-person perspective, as Duke of Gloucester

I, RICHARD PLANTAGENET II: LOYAULTE ME LIE. Second part of Richard's story, told in 1st person. The mystery of the Princes, the tragedy of Bosworth

A MAN WHO WOULD BE KING. First person account of Henry Stafford, Duke of Buckingham suspect in the murder of the Princes.

THE ROAD FROM FOTHERINGHAY—Richard III's childhood to his time in Warwick's household.

A VOUS ME LIE—Richard's youth in the household of Warwick the Kingmaker and beyond.

SACRED KING—Historical fantasy in which Richard III enters a fantastical afterlife and is 'returned to the world' in a Leicester carpark

WHITE ROSES, GOLDEN SUNNES. Collection of short stories about Richard III and his family.

SECRET MARRIAGES. Edward IV's romantic entanglements with Eleanor Talbot and Elizabeth Woodville

BLOOD OF ROSES. Edward IV defeats the Lancastrians at Mortimer's Cross and Towton.

RING OF WHITE ROSES. Two short stories featuring Richard III, including a time-travel tale about a lost traveller in the town of Bridport.

THE MISTLETOE BRIDE OF MINSTER LOVELL. Retelling of the folkloric tale featuring Francis Lovell, his wife and his friend the Duke of Gloucester.

Coming late 2022/early 2023—BROTHERS IN EXILE. Edward IV and Richard of Gloucester flee England as Warwick takes control and restores the Lancastrian Henry VI to the throne. Final book of the I, RICHARD PLANTAGENET SERIES

IN A SILVER SEA: REIMAGINED BRITISH LEGENDS

ENDELIENTA: Kinswoman of King Arthur. Endelienta seeks a mystic's life, living solely on the milk of mystical white cows.

MELOR OF THE SILVER HAND. A young lad has his hand and foot cut off by the uncle who would steal his throne—but with the aid of an ancient god with a hand of silver, Melor takes his revenge.

THE CROOKED ASH. The Derbyshire legend of Crooker. In the Middle Ages, a young man is called out to his sick mother. On the dark paths he meets three strange green-clad women—and the guardian of the ash tree.

THE BARROW WOMAN'S BONES—short ghost story set around a real archaeological find in Wiltshire.

DARK POOL, DARK MAIDEN—A haunting retelling of the Cornish tale of Lutey and the Mermaid.

STONEHENGE and prehistory:

THE STONEHENGE SAGA. Huge epic of the Bronze Age. Ritual, war, love and death. A prehistoric GAME OF STONES roughly based on the Arthurian legends but set in the British Bronze Age.

THE SWORD OF TULKAR-Collection of prehistoric-based short stories

THE GODS OF STONEHENGE-Short booklet about myths and legends associated with Stonehenge and about other possible mythological meanings.

MEDIEVAL BABES SERIES:

MY FAIR LADY: ELEANOR OF PROVENCE, HENRY III'S LOST QUEEN. One time-regent, her bones are lost in Amesbury.

MISTRESS OF THE MAZE: Rosamund Clifford, Mistress of Henry II. Was it murder? Did Eleanor of Aquitaine know?

THE CAPTIVE PRINCESS: Eleanor of Brittany, sister of the murdered Arthur, a prisoner of King John. Imprisoned for no crime save her royal blood.

THE WHITE ROSE RENT: The short life of Katherine, illegitimate daughter of Richard III

THE PRINCESS NUN. Mary of Woodstock, Daughter of Edward I, the nun who liked fun!

MY FATHER, MY ENEMY. Juliane, illegitimate daughter of Henry I, seeks to kill her father with a crossbow.

LONGSWORD'S LADY- Ela of Salisbury, married to William Longespee, half-brother to Richard I and King John. Found of Salisbury cathedral, female sheriff and powerful abbess.

POISONED CHALICE. The tale of Mabel de Belleme, Normandy's wicked lady, who poisoned her way to infamy.

THE OTHER MARGARET BEAUFORT. Margaret, Countess of Stafford, mother of Henry Stafford, Duke of Buckingham, suspect in the disappearance of the Princes in the Tower. Often confused with her more famous cousin, Margaret has her own tale to tell.

ROBIN HOOD

THE HOOD GAME:
1 Rise of the Green Wood King
2 Shadow of the Brazen Head
3 Blood of the Divine King.

Three-part historical fantasy series about the famous outlaw in a Sherwood Forest filled with spirits, old gods and magic. When young Robyn of Locksley wins 'the Hood' in an ancient winter rite, his life is changed forever.

Also, many short story collections and novellas of fantasy or historical fantasy.

Printed in Great Britain
by Amazon

20474310R00102